I0619045

INTRODUCTION TO THIS HOLIDAY MYSTERY!

A shocking attack. A terrible truth. Will our unseasoned baker burn the wrong bridges?

Cindy Claus enjoys her successful bakery business. She's finally proven to be more than the heir to her father's sleigh. But right in the middle of her busiest season, a panicked message from her regal mother threatens to destroy her dreams.

With Santa hovering on death's doorstep and Cindy delivering the presents this year, she'll need her new sleuthing skills and the help of her father's trusted arctic fox to save Saint Nic. But without a major holiday miracle, this could be the beginning of the end...

Can Cindy corner the culprit, or will this be the world's last Christmas?

Linzer Cookie Murder is the third book in the festive paranormal cozy series, Christmas Catastrophe Mysteries. If you like kind-hearted heroines, furry sidekicks, and a dash of mistletoe magic, then you'll love Trixie Silvertale's Yuletide puzzler.

Read *Linzer Cookie Murder* to wrap up a mystery today!

Features recipes from Cindy's bakery!

USA TODAY BESTSELLING AUTHOR

TRIXIE SILVERTALE

LINZER COOKIE MURDER

Christmas Catastrophe Mysteries

Copyright © 2025 by Trixie Silvertale

All rights reserved. Sittin' On A Goldmine Productions, L.L.C. and Trixie Silvertale reserve all rights to *Linzer Cookie Murder, Christmas Catastrophe Mysteries 3*. No part of this work may be reproduced, uploaded, scanned, distributed, or transmitted in any form or by any manner whatsoever, or stored in a database or retrieval system, without the prior written permission of the publisher, except for the use of brief quotations in a book review. Please purchase only authorized editions and do not participate in or encourage piracy of copyrighted materials. Your support of the author's rights is appreciated.

Sittin' On A Goldmine Productions, L.L.C.

pr@sittinonagoldmine.co

www.sittinonagoldmine.co

This is a work of fiction. Names, characters, places, and incidents are products of the author's imagination or are used fictitiously and are not to be construed as real. Any resemblance to actual events, locales, business establishments, organizations, or persons, living or dead, is entirely coincidental.

ISBN: 978-1-952739-24-8

Cover Design © Sittin' On A Goldmine Productions, L.L.C.

Trixie Silvertale
Linzer Cookie Murder: Paranormal Cozy Mystery : a novel / by Trixie Silvertale — 1st ed.
[1. Paranormal Cozy Mystery — Fiction. 2. Cozy Mystery — Fiction. 3. Amateur Sleuths — Fiction. 4. Female Sleuth — Fiction. 5. Wit and Humor — Fiction.] 1. Title.

CHAPTER 1

The refrain of "Jolly Old St. Nicholas" drifts up the sidewalk as a group of carolers, bundled against the cold, passes by.

"Blizzards! I already have my sign flipped to 'Closed.' Now they'll miss out on treats."

"Oh, geez." Keith Winters sets down his peppermint hot chocolate, swipes a hand through his high-and-tight black hair, and smiles. "Classic Cindy Claus. Of course you're worried about them not having treats. Catch 'em next time. You've been closed for over an hour. We were just getting into the good part of our end-of-the-day rap session."

His words are lost on me as I race behind the

pastry counter and load a large green pastry box with all the treats it can possibly hold.

My wild red hair slips from its messy bun, and I have to take a moment to scrape it back under control and into my Christmas-tree-print scrunchie.

I shove the overflowing box into Keith's hands. "Here! I'm sure you're faster than me. I can't use my elf—"

"Yip. Yip." My near slip of the tongue garners a warning from my father's most trusted advisor. A wise arctic fox named Artikoa, who sits in the foyer, where he's forced to play puppy dog.

When I convinced Papa — that's Santa Claus to you — that it wasn't my dream to deliver toys, but to leave the North Pole and open my own bakery, he agreed on the condition that Artikoa accompany me and keep me safe.

Initially, I didn't enjoy living with a spy. However, our relationship has progressed to a tentative friendship. But his current stance, with hackles raised, tells me he's in protector mode.

Keith's green eyes twinkle as he pops up from his chair and takes the pastry box. "I may not be an elf, but I'll get these delivered, Miss Claus." He chuckles at what he thinks is a joke. "And you better see what the emergency is with your pup, eh?"

The icy wind knifing across the great lake nestled on the shores of Silver Shoals ruffles Artikoa's snow-white fur as Keith races out the front door.

As soon as my human friend is out of earshot, Artikoa explodes with news. "Cynthia! Upstairs, at once."

Normally, I take issue with his bossy tone, but there's a tense urgency in his amber eyes. This is more than a scolding for a little slip of the tongue. It's almost as though there's a disturbance in the air. Taking the stairs two at a time, I turn on the creaking wooden landing, race up the second flight of stairs, and burst into my cozy studio apartment to find the snow globe on my bedside table glowing brightly with the image of my mother.

The elven queen is normally unflappable, but her current expression looks grave. "Cynthia! You must come home. At once!"

"Mama, things are going great in Silver Shoals. Yuletide Me Over Bakery is making a profit. That's what Artikoa tells me. And I have friends here." My shoulders lift against her command, but I attempt a casual chuckle.

"Cynthia, I have terrible news. Your father is quite ill. Please—" Her flawless features wrinkle with pain and tears flow from her green eyes.

Falling on my knees in front of the globe, I

grasp the glass bubble with both hands. "Mama, what's happened?"

"I've never seen him like this. You know he never gets sick. Now he's weak, and my magic isn't helping." She swipes at the falling tears. "Who will deliver the presents?"

That thought hadn't even occurred to me. This is probably one of the reasons I would make a terrible Santa. "Mama, what can I do? This is my busiest time of the year. I can't leave Jasmine alone. She makes amazing coffee drinks, but she doesn't know the first thing about baking. I'm sure Papa will be fine in a day or two."

My mother's tears cease abruptly and, even though she's thousands of miles away in a magically protected village at the North Pole, I feel the power in her voice as though she were standing beside me. "Cynthia Cherubim Claus, this isn't a discussion. Your queen requests your presence."

I can't refuse her. Plus, I'm worried about Papa. "Someone has to run my bakery, Mama. There are so many elves at the North Pole. Can you spare one? Can you send someone here to help in my bakery?"

Frustration pinches her fine features. She's not a woman used to negotiating. "I will send Cinnamon Roll. Will that suffice?"

A million thoughts are running through my

head, and I'm not a multitasker. I'll grab the most obvious one. "You have to do something about her ears. And there are so many human things — can you give me twenty-four hours?"

Her sparkling eyes blaze. "What are you saying?"

"Mama, I'm saying I'm worried about Papa and I'm going to help deliver presents, if it comes to that. But I need you to send Cinnamon Roll as soon as possible, and I need twenty-four hours to put things in order. I have a life here now, Mama. I can't just disappear."

My skin tingles as I feel her magic pulling against my flesh. "Mama, please."

In the blink of an eye, Cinnamon Roll, my baking mentor from the North Pole bakery, stands in the middle of my tiny apartment, and the snow globe falls dark.

Her pointed ears are curved round like a human's, and her expression is one of utter confusion. "Cindy? I didn't know you were in the North Pole." She fusses with her smudged apron, continues to look around the unfamiliar room, and crinkles her tiny button nose like a rabbit investigating its surroundings.

"CR!"

I throw my arms around her pudgy shoulders and hug her tight. The only thing that got me through the confusing years before I came clean with Santa about my bakery dreams was the delicious baked treats made by this amazing elf. "I'm not in the North Pole. You're in Silver Shoals. Mama sent you. I mean, Queen Erregina sent you."

CR offers me a friendly curtsy. "At your service, Your Highness."

I reach down and squeeze her shoulder. "None of that nonsense here. Papa is very ill. I have to return to the North Pole tomorrow, and I told Mama I needed someone to run my bakery. Can you do it? Can you help me out?"

She claps her hands together as though she's dusting flour from her palms. "Of course. Baking is baking. Whether it's in the North Pole or on this silver shelf."

Curling elf boots! It's taken me two years to learn a handful of these crazy human sayings and mannerisms. How can I possibly condense it all into one day? "It's Silver Shoals, Cinnamon. We better head down to the bakery right now. I have so many things to show you. Oh my stars, you will not believe how strange humans are!"

She reaches up and rubs her round ears. "Oh dear! What do you suppose happened to my ears?"

"The queen. I told her to fix them so you'd fit in."

"Done and dusted. Show me to your bakery, Cindy."

When I open the door and march onto the landing, I practically run down Keith.

He stops on the top step, looking from me to CR and back to me. "Whoa! How long was I gone?" Keith chuckles and spins the keys to his apartment on the index finger of his left hand.

Santa gave me this entire building as a Christmas present last year, so not only do I own the building my bakery resides in, I'm technically Keith's landlord. The fact that I'm sweet on him makes things even more complicated. I'm at an absolute loss for words.

Cinnamon Roll steps forward and curtsies. "Cinnamon Roll at your service. Are you also a baker?"

Keith's eyebrows pinch together, and he looks up at the ceiling for a moment before his sturdy gaze lands on me. "Cinnamon Roll. That name sounds familiar. Is she the woman who taught you how to bake?"

Before I can get a word in edgewise, my elven mentor is miles ahead. "Well, Cynthia's been working at the bakery since she was fifty-three. If she isn't the best baker in the North Pole, I don't know—"

"Yip. Yip. Yip. Yip."

Artikoa is going crazy, and CR has no idea why he's barking.

"Most Venerable Elder, are you choking?"

Icicles! This night could not get worse.

At last finding my voice, I step forward. "Cinnamon is just visiting. I need to show her something in the bakery. See you tomorrow. Oh, wait, I have to go home tomorrow. Oh dear! I've got to go."

Keith steps toward his door and shakes his head in confusion. "Nice to meet you, Cinnamon. I'm sure we'll catch up tomorrow. Is everything okay at home, Cindy?"

For the first time since my mother broke the news, the reality of my father's illness hits me like a frozen snowball. "My papa's very sick." The tears fly unbidden down my cheeks.

He's at my side in a flash and wipes my tears away. Keith wraps me in a hug, while CR looks on in complete shock. Her tiny elven jaw hangs open like an abandoned oven door.

Artikoa noses her toward the stairs, and luckily she follows him down to the bakery.

"Geez, I'm so sorry to hear about your dad, Cindy. Please let me know if there's anything I can do."

"I'd be most appreciative if you could help Cinnamon. I do have to leave tomorrow. And I just won't have time to teach her everything about hu — huge bakery trends."

He rolls his athletic shoulders back and laughs. "Huge bakery trends? Not sure I can be much help there. But I'll do my best. You get downstairs and show her whatever you can. I'll do everything in my power to assist her while you're away." He lightly kisses my cheek, and my Claus skin immediately turns rosy.

"Um, thanks." More blushing.

He smiles warmly as he unlocks his door. "Don't leave without saying goodbye, eh?"

It feels as though my face may be glowing. "Okay. Sure. You bet." My mouth keeps running as I stumble down the stairs.

That smile . . .

CHAPTER 2

A smart girl probably would've gotten a good night's rest before attempting to teach a North Pole elf everything there is to know about humans in less than twenty-four hours. Thing is, I'm only one quarter "girl." The other quarter is angel, and then I'm half elf. And we elves do love to be busy.

The minute I walk through the doors of the bakery and catch sight of Cinnamon whispering to Artikoa, it's obvious I'm in trouble.

"I hate to say it, but it looks as though you two are scheming."

Cinnamon Roll spins on her tiny curled boots and giggles like an elf half her age. "Tell me about this human. This Keith Winters. Most Venerable Elder Artikoa says he's a special friend."

Clearly, my father's trusted advisor has spilled more than his share of secrets in the thirty seconds it took me to get down the stairs.

My mother always used to tell me I would protest too much when I defended myself. Probably best to come clean.

"Not that it's *any* of anyone's business, but Keith is a medical investigator for the local sheriff's department. He's naturally kind and he's always trusted me. When I was accused of murder, he told me he believed I was innocent. Plus, I've helped him solve two cases. And, well, he comes into the bakery almost every night after I close. When he's not working on a case, I mean. We share a peppermint hot chocolate and he tells me about his day, and he asks about my day." After a sharp inhale, I bite my lip and announce, "Call me crazy, but I think he might be more than a special friend."

Artikoa's puffy backside abruptly hits the floor, and he stares in that unnerving, unblinking way of a true predator.

CR, on the other hand, rushes forward and grips my hands between her small, calloused fingers. "Oh, Cindy! I'm as pleased as a mama reindeer with twins! Your story reminds me of how I met Barrel."

Over the many years I worked in her bakery, I'd met Mr. Roll several times, but I don't think I'd ever heard his first name. "And what was it that attracted you to Barrel?"

She squeezes my hand so tight my fingers begin to tingle.

"Kindness, dear. His immense capacity for kindness. That and the fact that he makes the best cup of peppermint hot chocolate I've ever had the pleasure of drinking." She blushes and giggles. "If you ask me, this Keith Winters sounds like the perfect Christmas present. One that you would never, ever think about returning."

Artikoa remains silent, but his gaze softens.

"What do you say, MVE? Do you approve of me taking things to the next level with Mr. Winters?"

"My priorities are to get the Christmas presents safely delivered and your father back on his feet. Then we can speak of this romantic non-sense." He chuffs air through his narrow nose.

CR drops one of my hands, and the circulation comes rushing back in prickles.

"Let's finish the tour, Cindy. You can tell me more about this divine human while we're baking."

My cheeks flush to brightest red. I can almost picture them dwarfing my father's most famous reindeer's nose!

"Thanks for understanding, CR." I exhale a huge sigh of relief and gesture to the bakery. "So, this is Yuletide Me Over Bakery. My pride and joy."

"Oh, Cindy! It's just lovely. I can't believe how much space you have! And this red and gold lettering on the window is perfect! Look at your gleaming pastry case! Are those baskets on the wall for fresh bread? All this is yours?" She ducks her head into the back room. "There's more?" CR claps her hands eagerly. "Let's get started. Looks like you have absolutely everything we need. Where do you keep the reindeer milk?"

Taking a deep breath, I launch into lesson number one about the human world. Pulling out my North Pole recipes, I show CR all the substitutions I've made. Then I retrieve the cookbooks passed down to me by my dearly-departed landlord, Ronnie Schmenkel. These special recipes belonged to his late wife, Connie. I push thoughts of Ronnie's murder from my mind and struggle to focus on the task at hand.

"As you can see, we'll have to make some adjustments. Tomorrow I'll take you down to the

Piggly Wiggly and show you where to get supplies. I have an account there, so you won't need any money."

"You have your own greenhouse?"

"What?"

"You said something about a wiggling pig. Does that mean you're not a vegetarian? Or is that what you call your greenhouse?"

"Aurora borealis! CR, I don't know how I can take everything I've learned in the last two years and cram it into a twenty-four-hour lesson. The most useful things I can tell you are: Humans love sarcasm. Most don't grow any of their own food. You have to have money for everything here." I reach into my pocket and pull out some green-and-white paper. "Use these bills to pay for everything you want. No trades. No bartering."

Cinnamon Roll scrunches up her round face, and her large brown eyes seem to drift off and lose focus. "Aha. And you do this? Pay for things?"

"Yep. That's how it works."

Artikoa steps forward. "Cynthia, if I may interject. It would be best if you show Cinnamon all you can about the bakery. I've never observed such agitation in Queen Erregina. The sooner we transport you back to the North Pole, the better."

My first instinct is to defend my independence,

but there's a concern in Artikoa's voice that softens my defense mechanism. "You're right. Mama was very upset. Let's get to baking, CR!"

She adjusts her little apron and smiles from formerly pointed ear to formerly pointed ear. "Now you're talking."

After a quick tour of the kitchen — ingredients, pans, ovens, and recipes — we get to work.

When my assistant, Jasmine, walks into the bakery in the morning, the pastry cases are full, and the second batch of dough for the afternoon's gooey caramel cinnamon rolls is already in the proofing drawer.

Jasmine's low whistle reaches our ears before she rounds the corner. Whatever she was planning on saying sticks in her throat like an underbaked cookie. Her big dark eyes take in the scene, and she arches one eyebrow. "Am I out of a job?"

I hope there's no guilt in my blue eyes. "No. Never. I can explain."

She laughs and waves her hands. "JK, Cindy. Who's your friend?"

Before answering, I lean down and whisper to CR, "JK means just kidding. It's part of that sarcasm and humor I was trying to explain."

CR widens her bright eyes and offers a much belated chuckle.

"Jasmine, this is my—" Oops. I can't lie. And I can't exactly tell her the truth. "My friend who taught me how to bake. This is Cinnamon Roll."

Jasmine reaches out her hand. "Cool nickname."

CR stares blankly at the outstretched hand and — looking up at Jasmine — widens her smile. "Nickname?"

Jingle bells! My Christmas goose is well and truly cooked. Reaching out, I shake Jasmine's hand. "Cinnamon Roll, this is Jasmine. She works out front and makes the most amazing coffee drinks."

CR, noting the exchange, juts her left hand outward and says, "Cool nickname."

Jasmine scrunches up her face, shakes her head, and laughs as she turns and walks into the retail space.

CR smiles at me with an innocence I used to possess.

"Cinnamon, when humans stick out their hand like that, you have to grab it with your right hand and shake it." I demonstrate for her. "It's their favorite greeting. I have no idea why. But you have to do it if you want to fit in."

She nods her head. "No problem." She thrusts her right hand out and I shake it as I giggle.

"You don't have to do it all the time. Just when

you first meet someone. And nickname means not your real name. It's like a special name that someone might call you. Like I call Jasmine 'Jazz' for short. Plus, I call you CR. That's kind of a nickname."

CR squeezes her eyes to narrow slits and purses her tiny rose petal mouth. "But Cinnamon Roll *is* my name."

"I know. It's hard for humans. They're not used to the different types of names we have at the North Pole. Elf names and human names are not exactly the same. Do you understand?"

She shakes her head and shrugs her little round shoulders. "Not a bit. But if you say it's true, I believe you. Elves can't lie."

Nodding my head, I untie my apron and announce, "Let's head down to the grocery store. That's the Piggly Wiggly that we talked about earlier. I'll show you how to find all the ingredients, and we can talk to Mitch. He owns the store. I'll tell him to put your name on my account. That way, you won't have to worry about taking money with you when you need to pick up supplies."

She puts one hand on her full hip. "Money is the green-and-white paper. And I have to use that to pay for things . . . Because humans don't like to barter."

"Sounds good to me, CR. Let's hit the road."

Hanging my green apron on the hook, I let Jasmine know where we're headed. Artikoa has vanished, but I can almost picture him upstairs chatting with my mother through the magical snow globe.

No time to worry about that mess.

CHAPTER 3

*A*s CR and I breeze down the sidewalk toward the grocery store, I throw information at her like the loading elves tossing presents into Santa's magic bag. For a North Pole elf who's never left the protection of my mother's magic dome, CR is taking it all in stride. "So these cars, they drive on that part of the sidewalk, and we walk on this part of the sidewalk. Is that right?"

Stifling a chuckle, I encourage her to the best of my abilities. "You're doing great. The part the cars drive on is called 'the road,' and the part the people, or elves, walk on is called 'the sidewalk.' As long as you stay on this part, here, you'll be okay."

She nods. "Done and dusted."

"Now we have to cross the street. This is very

important." I reach out and grip her hand as though she were a small human child. "Whenever you cross the street, you have to check both directions for those cars. They drive kind of fast around here, and it would be very dangerous if one of them hit you."

Her small smile straightens. "Got it. Always check for cars. My goodness, Cindy. How did you learn all of this? Seems like you've only been gone for a few months."

We hurry across the street and through the parking lot toward the Piggly Wiggly. "It's actually been two years. And it was difficult. I had a lot of help from Ronnie Schmenkel. He was a kind man who passed away last year. He used to own the building Papa—" Tears spring from my eyes.

CR tugs at my hand. As I bend down, she throws her arms around me and offers comfort. "You sweet thing. I didn't mean to make you cry. I don't really understand what happened to Ronnie."

Before we enter the store, I give her an incredibly brief explanation of the fragility of humans, their short lifespans, and their funeral customs.

For the first time since she abruptly landed in Silver Shoals, she looks shocked.

"My goodness! How tragic." Her strong fingers press to her lips. "Well, I'm sure our baked goods will at least bring them some joy in their painfully brief lives."

The magic doors slide open, and CR squeals with delight. "Jingle bells! They do have some magic."

There's no point in bursting her bubble.

"That's the thing about humans. Even though their lives are so short, they find ways to squeeze out every drop of joy. It's actually pretty impressive."

She scrunches up her face and winks. "I can see why your father is so taken with them."

The thought had never occurred to me. I'd always assumed my father loved to make and deliver toys. Hadn't really thought about the fact that he'd have to actually like humans to want to visit every one of their homes every year on Christmas Eve. Interesting. Seems like I do have something in common with my father.

CR and I are pushing the cart down the aisle, and I'm pointing to which ingredients she'll need to know how to identify, when the store owner, Mitch, emerges from the back room. He has a lovely reindeer-brown mustache and a welcome smile. "Cindy! Who is this? A friend or a relative?"

"This is my good friend, Cinnamon. She taught me everything I know about baking."

Mitch surges forward and extends his hand.

To CR's credit, she's ready for it. She grips his hand and shakes it fiercely. "Nice to meet you, Mitch."

He leans back and drags his hand from hers. "Nice to meet you as well. If you had anything to do with teaching Cindy how to make such delightful baked goods, you're definitely one of my heroes."

An easy blush touches her cheeks as she shakes off the compliment. "Oh, I didn't teach her anything. She was born with magic."

Fortunately, humans don't believe in magic, and Mitch simply thinks she's paying me a compliment. "You've got that right, Cinnamon. Can I help you ladies find anything?"

She chuckles. "I'd love to get my hands on some reindeer milk if you have it."

His eyes widen, and his wrinkled brow tugs his eyebrows up in a strange curve. "Is that some new hipster trend? I've never heard of it."

I leap into the middle of this disaster. "She's kidding, Mitch. I'm just showing her the ropes. She's going to take care of the bakery for a few days while I go home for a visit."

He tilts his head with interest. "How wonderful. And where's home?"

Frozen snowballs! I should've seen that coming.

Thankfully, CR is getting the hang of things. "Oh, it's way up north, Mitch."

We all share a friendly laugh, and he hurries to the register to attend to a customer.

She looks up at me with her indigo-blue eyes. "It certainly is difficult to be among humans and not tell a lie. How have you managed?"

"I haven't managed that well at all. Lucky for me, humans don't believe in things like the North Pole or magic or being 117 years old. So when I've made mistakes, they assume it's a joke. But it has been tricky. Especially with people I'm close to." My gaze drifts off as I think of dreamy Keith.

We finish making the rounds in the store, and I feel confident CR will be able to manage things while I'm away. At least in the bakery!

When we check out, Mitch adds her name to my account and assures me she'll have no problem buying ingredients while I'm away.

"Thank you, Mitch. That's very reassuring. Have a lovely day."

I push the cart toward the front door, and he calls after us, "I always do!"

As we make our way back toward Yuletide Me Over Bakery, I gesture to the laundromat, which leads to an explanation of doing laundry, and the cranky owner, Todd. As we pass the hardware store, I assure her she won't need anything from there.

Before we take the turnoff to the alley behind the bakery, I make sure to point out the vegetarian restaurant and let her know how many delicious things she can find there.

"You'll need some of the green-and-white paper when you go there. I don't have an account with them. You'll have to pay each time you order food."

"Don't worry about me. I could survive on cookies and mini cheesecakes for weeks at a time!"

We both chuckle, and she helps me carry the groceries up the concrete steps and through the back door into the kitchen.

No sooner have we brought in the last bag of groceries than Artikoa bursts into the kitchen — which he never does during business hours — so I'm concerned even before he yips.

"Yip. Yip."

He nods his sharply pointed nose toward the apartment above, and I quickly follow him. It's another call from Mama. She's distraught. "Cynthia, you must come home at once. Your father is worse. Much worse. I can't—"

There's no need for her to finish the sentence. My recent experiences with human death can easily fill in the blanks. She's concerned my half angel and half human father may be reaching the end of his unnaturally long life span.

Glancing around the room, I shrug my shoulders and lock eyes with Artikoa. "Can you stay behind? At least for another day or two? I have to go now, and Cinnamon still—"

"As you wish, Princess."

"Thanks, Arti." It always throws me when he calls me princess. But it's not a derogatory term. I literally am royalty. "Arti, can you ask Cinnamon to say goodbye to Keith for me? I feel bad leaving without talking to him."

"Of course." He nods once.

Turning to the snow globe, I take a deep breath and announce, "I'm ready, Mama. Bring me home."

In a flash, Silver Shoals vanishes.

CHAPTER 4

*I*n the blink of an elf's eye, I'm back in my bedroom at the North Pole. The feeling of home is squashed by a wave of claustrophobia. I can almost feel the protective dome pressing in around me.

"Cynthia!" My mother's arms are around me, and her tears soak into my Christmas tree sweater.

"Mama, don't cry. Papa will be fine. He's healthy as a polar bear. It's surely just a case of the sniffles."

She leans back. Her thick golden curls are missing their inner light, and — I would never tell her — it looks as though she's put on some weight. Mama sniffs sharply to mask her emotions, and brushes away her tears. "Come, Cynthia. Your father will be so comforted to see you."

Mama leads me to the north end of our sprawling home.

When she opens the door to their bedroom — nothing could have prepared me.

Papa, propped up on several pillows, lies motionless in the bed. His eyelids slowly open, but the jolly sparkle has gone from his dark eyes. His normally rosy cheeks are nearly ashen. My chest squeezes tight as I rush forward. "I'm home, Papa. I'm here."

A limp arm drapes over my shoulder, and a breathy voice whispers, "My Marshmallow."

I'm powerless to hold back my tears. I didn't want to cry in front of him, but I never expected to see him like this.

He continues in his raspy, strained tones, "Don't cry, Marshmallow. It's just a little touch of the flu. I'll be good as new in a couple days. You can help me load the sleigh."

"Papa, you're in no condition— I'll do it. I'll deliver the toys, Papa. You can count on me."

Like a flash of quicksilver, the sparkle of life zips through his eyes. Then it's gone. "Thank you, Cindy. That's probably best."

His arm slides from my shoulder and falls motionless at his side. His eyelids flutter closed, and his breath continues in a raspy rhythm.

My mother steps forward and grips my shoulder. "Come downstairs, Cynthia. We can talk there."

As I place a kiss on my father's forehead, I glance at the half-eaten plate of cookies on his bedside table. Perfect little Linzer cookie sandwiches. Shiny raspberry jam peeks through a Christmas-tree-shaped cutout, and a dusting of powdered sugar covers the golden surface.

While Mama and I walk downstairs, I have to ask. "He's still eating cookies? In his condition?"

Mama exhales dramatically. "You know your father this time of year, Cynthia. You can't get the cookies away from him. I've made healing potions and hearty vegetable stews, but he'll hardly take two bites." She waves her thin arms in frustration. "Cookies. It's always cookies." When we reach the bottom of the steps, she heads to the stove to put the kettle on for tea.

"Mama, can I make us peppermint hot chocolate?"

"Make some for yourself, dear. I'm fine with herbal tea."

Sitting across the table, as we have so many times over the last hundred plus years, this is the first time I've ever seen my mother's shoulders slump in defeat.

"You said you made some healing potions for him. Have any of them helped?"

"You saw what he looked like. Nothing's working. He's been getting worse for nearly two weeks. I keep hoping he will turn a corner and the light will come back to his eyes. I fear this may be the end, Cynthia." An anguished sob rips from her throat, and she drops her head into her arms on the table.

Confused and frightened, I rub my hand on her back and wonder what I can possibly do. "We should both try to get some sleep. In the morning, I'll go down to the factory and see where we're at with the production numbers. Then I'll check in with the reindeer wranglers and make sure the team is ready to go. What about the new recruits? Anything I should know there?"

My mother's head lifts a few inches, and her red-rimmed eyes look up at me with a flicker of hope. "I don't know anything. I've been so worried about your father . . . I've ignored my duties. I'm a terrible queen."

Sliding from my chair, I slip my arms around her and hug her tight. "You don't need to be a queen right now. You're a wonderful wife and mother. You're doing the very best you can. Let me walk you upstairs, Mama."

At the top of the stairs, when I attempt to turn toward her room, she pushes back and shakes her head. "I've been sleeping in your room, Cynthia. I can't bear to see him like this."

"That's okay, Mama. I'm happy to share my room with you. Let's get a little shuteye, okay?"

She leans heavily, and I can feel her weariness as I help her remove her outer robes, guide her into bed, and pull the covers over her shoulders.

Despite her protests, she falls into a fitful sleep as soon as her head hits the pillow.

NOTES OF "JINGLE BELLS" BLAST from the North-Pole-wide intercom system. Must be 5:00 a.m. I'm recalling the many reasons I left the North Pole.

The last few days before Christmas are pure chaos.

I roll over to discover my mother has vacated her spot and carefully made her half of the large, round bed. Not wanting to stir up trouble on my first proper day home, I follow suit and straighten the sheets, blankets, and comforter on my side as well.

A quick peek into Papa's room shows an empty cookie plate next to his bedside, and a light snoring coming from under the thick, red-velvet duvet.

When I tiptoe downstairs, a healthy egg-white omelette and a handful of fresh blueberries from the greenhouse await me.

My mother looks more herself today. She's in her workout clothes, and her flaxen hair is smoothly caught in a high ponytail. "Will you be joining me for yoga this morning, Cynthia?"

"No, Mama. I need to head straight to the factory. I have no idea where things are at." Her face falls, and I quickly add, "Thank you for inviting me. And thank you for this wonderful breakfast. It's exactly what I need to get my day off on the right foot."

My approval of her healthy offering brings a brief smile to her lips. She grabs her yoga mat and exits gracefully.

I force down my healthy morning meal and sip at something that isn't coffee. Possibly yerba maté? My mother loves trying exotic new things.

After washing my dishes, I head out.

Wandering down the cobblestone streets of my once home, there's an odd comfort in the ever-sameness. Each shop is brightly lit, and the signs are freshly painted. The cobblestones in the streets are so clean they appear to have been scrubbed by hand only yesterday.

Between you and me, magic is what keeps everything looking so spiffy. It's the reason I had so little information on cleaning and doing laundry when I headed out on my own. It wasn't something I'd ever had to deal with. As I pass Cinnamon Roll's bakery, I can't contain my curiosity or my appetite for sweets. Biting my lip, I hesitate and promise myself I'll pop in and only have a quick gingerbread cookie.

When I push open the door, Cinnamon Roll's daughter, Jelly, nearly jumps over the counter. "Cindy! I received a letter from your mother. Apparently my mother went to take care of your bakery. Are you here to work at ours?"

Chuckling, I approach the counter and smile warmly at Jelly. "I'm so sorry about all of this. Please don't tell anyone, but my father is very ill. I had to come home to take care of delivering the presents on Christmas Eve. And your—"

"Santa is sick?!?" Jelly's sweet face pales.

"Yes. Please don't say anything. I'm sure he'll be fine in a day or two. He just can't run the sleigh. I didn't feel comfortable leaving my bakery unattended, so your mother headed into the human world to help me out. Are you okay here?

Do you need me to find someone else to help you?"

No sooner have I posed the question than an elf I don't recognize wanders from the back.

Jelly turns toward her and exhales with relief. "Thank you, but we're fine. This is Willow. She's been helping at the bakery for the last few weeks. And she is a dab hand. My mother was so impressed with how quickly she learned the recipes. Willow knows how to make all of our best cookies. She still hasn't learned the secret family cinnamon roll recipe, but you know you have to work here at least a year before Mother will share that one." Jelly puts a hand on her tummy and snorts.

"Oh, I remember. And, I'll tell you what, it was absolutely worth every day of that year, Willow. Good luck to you."

Willow smiles nervously and wanders forward.

"I didn't catch your name." Her tone isn't exactly friendly.

"I'm Cindy. Cindy Claus."

Her face shifts toward expressionless and her mouth moves, but no words come out. Jelly jumps to defend her. "Don't be upset, Cindy. You've been gone for almost two years. Not everyone knows you like before."

I wave away their concerns. "It's no big deal. I've never expected you to treat me like a princess.

I have no problem introducing myself. Very nice to meet you, Willow."

She tilts her head down and lowers her gaze. "An honor to meet you, Your Highness."

"There'll be none of that. When I'm in the bakery, I'm Cindy. Got it?"

She still avoids making eye contact. "Yes, Your Highness. Cindy. Yes." With that, Willow wrings her hands nervously and hurries into the back. "I need to help Violet with the cinnamon rolls."

"And don't forget the deliveries. You two work it out." Jelly shrugs her shoulders and giggles. "Give her some time. Willow is pretty shy for an elf."

I open my mouth to ask a follow-up question, but the front door bursts open and a familiar face darkens the door.

"Can I get a pound of acorns?" The hunched elf teeters as he tugs his tattered cloak over bony shoulders.

Jelly covers her mouth with one round hand and stifles a giggle. "Still no acorns, Mr. Winkle. You want the shop across the street."

The ancient elf blows a raspberry and rubs a gnarled finger over his cracked lips. "Been buyin' 'em here for a hundred years."

My turn. "Mr. Winkle, you said our prices were

too high. The young elf across the street at Go Nuts for Less gives you a better price."

Mr. Winkle grumbles. "That sounds like me. Thank you, Cindy."

As soon as the door closes behind him, Jelly and I have a fit of giggles.

"Wacky Winkle still comes in here for acorns? After all these years?" Of course, Wacky isn't his actual name. I have no idea what it is. Cinnamon Roll and I started calling him Wacky Winkle as an inside joke after his twentieth attempt to buy acorns.

Jelly bobs her head and wipes tears of laughter from her rosy cheeks. "Yup. I'll have to remember that answer you gave him. That shortened the debate by at least ten minutes."

Sighing with the sweet sting of memories, I reply, "At least *he* remembered me."

Her eyes widen as she nods. "He did! Now what can I get you?"

I order my gingerbread cookies (yes that's plural) with an extra side of icing, and struggle to hide my building excitement as Jelly puts my order together.

"Two helpers? Business must be booming."

Jelly blushes as she squares her shoulders. "They're both fairly new. My sweet mother has never hired outside the family before. It's almost as though she knew she'd be leaving for a bit."

Arching my eyebrow, I give the comment serious consideration. "But that's impossible — isn't it?"

"Nothing is impossible at the North Pole, Cindy." She winks.

Thanking Jelly, I walk out of the bakery, pondering the impossible.

CHAPTER 5

*I*t seems hard to believe I've only been away from the North Pole for two years. Here I am, about to celebrate my 118th birthday, and I feel more like a visitor than someone who used to live here.

Eating as I wander, I wend my way toward the factory — and duty.

Rounding the last corner, I receive quite a surprise. A group of elves, each holding small hand-painted signs with intricate gold filigree lettering, march in front of the entrance to the factory.

Pausing out of sight, I rely on my sharp elven eyes to read the signs. I assumed they would be filled with messages of cheer and encouragement. What I behold shocks me to my core.

"Elven Rights Mean Sleep At Night!"

"If Santa Loves Toys So Much, Why Doesn't HE Make Them?!"

"Return To The Forest! No More Factories!"

I've never seen anything like this in my life. How can elves be unhappy at Christmas? There must be some mistake. I sure hope nothing is wrong at the factory. Mama has been overwhelmed taking care of Papa. This is the last thing she needs.

Taking a cautious breath, I step into the street to confront the protesters and get to the bottom of this un-elvenly display.

Wacky Winkle and his wheelbarrow of acorns come out of nowhere. He knocks me off my feet — purely by accident — and my head hits the cobblestone harder than a racing reindeer hoof.

A presence hunches over me, smelling of earth and acorns, as visions of protesters dance behind my closed eyes. Blinking, I search the dimly lit room for anything familiar.

Bundles of herbs hung from the rafters to dry.

Sacks of acorns on every flat surface.

A thin clothesline, seeming to hold the bed-posts upright, displays two pair of ancient under-garments.

I have no idea how much time has passed. "Mama?"

Wacky Winkle totters into the room and places a mug on the crooked bedside table. "Drink some acorn tea. It's good for everything. A thousand apologies for running you down, Your Highness. Can I make you an acorn butter sandwich?"

I had absolutely no idea that Wacky Winkle actually ate the acorns he's always in search of.

"Thank you, Wa— Mr. Winkle. I best be getting home. Mama will be— Queen Erregina will be worried."

At the mention of Mama's formal title, he bends one knobby knee to me and smiles. "Indeed. And she will always be my queen. Despite the ramblings of my clan."

"What do you mean, Mr. Winkle? What's going on with your clan?"

He gestures to the tea and scrapes a three-legged stool closer to the bedside.

"You drink your tea, dearie, and I'll tell you what I know."

Scooting myself up against the lumpy pillow, I bring the steaming mug of tea to my lips and take a tentative sip.

Hmmmm. It's kind of tasty. Not as delicious as mother's chamomile and lavender tea or hibiscus ginger tea, but it's pleasant. Settling against the rough pillow, I sip the tea and listen to Winkle's tale.

"The forest clan is ruled by Sequoia, the second oldest elf in the North Pole, and the eldest elf in the forest clan. She's always been levelheaded, generous, and stern with upstarts.

"Offspring came to her late in life, and I reckon this led her to overindulge what she saw as a miracle. When gentle Sequoia passed from us earlier this year, she was planted in the small forest to the west. A wee sapling has begun to sprout there." He coughs, and a deep rattle in his chest shakes his frail body.

"Can I make you some tea, Mr. Winkle?"

"You took quite a lump on the head, dearie. Stay put. Old Winkle has a remedy for this cough." He reaches into the pocket of his tattered cloak and removes a small tincture bottle. When he pops the cap, the smell of mullein, eucalyptus, and honey wafts toward me.

He takes two small sips and returns the bottle to his cloak. "Where was I?"

"Um, I believe you were at the sapling."

He wets his lips and leans back. "Before that sapling was knee high to a reindeer, Sequoia's rebellious son, Ash, took the reins. None stood against him. They trusted in the long peaceful history that Sequoia had handed down." Winkle blows a low whistle and shakes his head.

"Within a month, Ash came a-stirring the embers and attempting to light the forest clan aflame. He cited our numbers. He cited our loss of habitat." Winkle gazes into the distance, and a mournful tone tints his raspy voice. "The old-growth forests of eastern and northern Europe were a thing of beauty." An ache weakens his voice. "The dangers of the barbarians far outweighed the beauty of those trees."

"Mr. Winkle, did you fight against the barbarian hoards?"

His milky eyes gaze at the floor, and a shudder runs over his body as though invisible forces grab his shoulders and shake him.

"Those were dark days, dearie. Horrible acts were committed in the name of protection. No matter how deeply I long for the old forests, I could never return. I've seen too much. Endured atrocities I'd hoped to never—" He presses a gnarled hand to his throat and draws a ragged breath. "We don't speak of them. We prefer the details remain lost to the ages."

His crackling voice chokes with emotion, and he hobbles to his kitchen to make himself a cup of tea. When he returns, I smell chamomile and valerian.

"Mr. Winkle, I'm so sorry to have upset you. I hope the tea brings you comfort."

He nods his craggy face and wipes a tear from

under his left eye. "I fear I rely too heavily on the aid of valerian these days. As I reach the end of my journey on this side of the dirt, I wish to push the bad times into the background and focus my remaining memories on the good."

My mug of tea is nearly empty, and I'm certain Anise will be wondering why I'm not at the factory. If anyone mentions it to Mama, she'll be upset.

"Mr. Winkle, I must be going. Queen Erregina will worry."

"Of course, dearie. Give your mother my allegiance. I may not be the leader of my clan, but I remain a venerable elder. I will do what I can."

Getting to my feet, I slip on my curved elf boots and smile at the simple joys of the North Pole. "You think this young upstart, Ash, will cause more trouble? What does he hope to achieve?"

"The youngster wants to unify the forest clan and return to Europe. He says the only way forward is to fracture the peace we cherish in this idyllic place. He believes we're growing weak. The elfling has never known true suffering. He speaks with the innocence and naïveté of youth."

My throat tightens, and tears leak from my eyes. Reaching out, I grip Mr. Winkle's gnarled hand. "Do you think — he would ever try to hurt my father?"

A fiery defiance fills the ancient elf's eyes. "Dearie, the clans would've passed into oblivion if not for the sanctuary your father helped create. Ash wouldn't dare."

"Thank you for the tea, Mr. Winkle. And for nursing me back to health."

As I walk toward the door, he calls in a raspy voice like crinkling newspaper, "Beg your pardon for running you down on the boulevard, dearie."

"None needed, Mr. Winkle."

As I venture onto the street, I feel utterly lost. Mr. Winkle's home is tucked into a twisted dead end off the main cobblestone street.

I have no memory of visiting any of these strange shops. When I reach the corner, the bakery glows happily on the opposite side of the street. "Okay, now I know where I am."

Better head to the factory and get my day back on track. Perhaps I'll keep this information about the forest clan to myself for now. No need to put more worries on Mama's plate.

As I pass the crumbled remains of my sugar-cookie icing cup, a sharp pain flares in my left leg. That cart of acorns hit me harder than I thought. Hopefully, my elf and angel blood will get busy healing the ache in my noggin, as well as this new pain.

Keeping my head down, I skirt the protesters, slip through the front doors of the factory and scan the earnest faces for Anise.

Once I'm recognized, panic spreads like an early spring thaw. Elves run hither and yon, and, within seconds, an announcement goes out over the PA.

"Stations, everyone. Cynthia Claus is in the building."

Oh, cookie crumbs. So much for keeping things casual.

"Hello, Anise. How's production going?"

There's a visible gulp as she takes a deep breath. "We're on schedule, Miss Claus. You can count on us. The loaders are prepping Santa's bag, and we will take the final numbers tomorrow night. Everything is under control here. Perhaps you should head out and meet the reindeer. There've been quite a few changes since you left."

"Thank you. I'm so glad you have everything in hand. That will certainly make my job easier. If that's possible." I scrunch my shoulders up and smile, hoping to send the message that we're all in this together.

Leaving the factory, I breathe a sigh of relief and head toward the stables.

News of my presence in the North Pole reaches the reindeer wranglers before I arrive. They have the entire team lined up and harnessed for inspection. "Good morning, good elves."

One bows, and one offers a small curtsy as they reply in unison. "Good morning, Your Highness."

Clearly there's no getting around the formalities. "Is this the team that will be pulling the sleigh?"

"Yes, Miss. Unless you want to make any changes." The duet of their voices is unnerving.

"Oh no. I absolutely trust your judgment. You work with these beautiful creatures every day. I'm sure you know best."

The elves again speak in unison. "Thank you for saying so, Miss."

As I look over the elves, I note they appear to be identical twins. Although one is perhaps a girl and one a boy, they are indistinguishable.

"I trust you two have figured out a way to get them into the air. As far as I know, I don't have my father's touch."

They both turn. "Don't fret, Miss. On Christmas Eve, all things are possible."

"Wonderful. Can I see the new recruits?"

This request was clearly not something they were expecting. They exchange frantic glances and both swallow hard.

"I can come back later if now isn't a good time. It's not a problem."

They answer in unison. "No, Miss. Give us two shakes of an arctic hare's tail. We'll put the team away and take you on a tour." The only evidence of their discomfort is that they end their little speech about a syllable apart. Almost as though there was an echo in the space.

"Perfect. I'll wait right here."

Zipping around with inhuman speed, they unharness the team and return each of the lead reindeer to their comfortable stalls. Less than two minutes have passed when they stand in front of me, bouncing on the toes of their curving boots. "Sorry for the wait, Miss. Follow us."

The twins turn in perfect sync and walk me into the stables. As they show me each of the yearlings sent over by the tribe of reindeer living outside the North Pole's protective bubble, I can see why they are so proud of the new bunch. "What a beautiful group of recruits! How many did they send this year?"

Turning, the twins reply, "Ten, Miss. Per Santa's request."

Glancing over my shoulder, I make a quick mental count. I only remember seeing nine, but, after the stress I've already put them under, I don't want to send any more shockwaves through the stables today.

"Thank you for that lovely tour. I look forward

to seeing you again on Christmas Eve. Please let me know if you need anything from me before that."

The twins bounce one more time and smile broadly. "You can count on us, Your Highness."

CHAPTER 6

$\mathcal{A}$ ll of this North Pole excitement has put me in the mood to bake cookies. Papa seems to be on a Linzer cookie trend, but I'm sure he'd appreciate some of my homemade ginger-bread cookies. Those always were his favorite.

Hurrying home, I pull out ingredients, and I'm surprised to find no ginger root in the cupboard. I'll have to head out to the greenhouses and dig up my own. That's okay. Fresh is best!

Heading the opposite direction of the bakery, I bypass the cozy community center, which is absolutely empty this time of year. Every one at the North Pole is either working double shifts at the factory or double shifts in one of the vital businesses that keep all the elves clothed and fed.

When I reach the greenhouses, there are several elves busily working to keep the crops healthy and productive.

I wave, and a couple of the workers smile, but there's no wave of recognition, a bow, or a curtsy. After being away from here for two years, it's a strange feeling to *want* to be treated like royalty again.

Entering the greenhouse where the ginger grows, I grab a spade off the table by the door and locate the row. As I carefully extract two rhizomes from the ginger root, my gaze wanders to the greenhouse behind the one I currently occupy. My mother's private gardens. From where I'm sitting, the padlock appears to be open.

I finish removing the rhizomes from the ginger plant, pat down the soil, and return the spade to the table where I found it. Always keep things tidy and neat. That's the elf's way. I hate to admit it, but the lessons of my childhood seem to take over up here at the North Pole.

I'm glad to have the chance to pop in and say hi to Mama before I start baking. Skirting around the perimeter of the large greenhouse, I approach the smaller, private structure.

Opening the door I call out, "Mama? Where are you? I just wanted to say hello before I make a batch of cookies for Papa." No reply.

Quickly traversing the aisles, I find no sign of my mother. Perhaps she left in a hurry. She seems so distracted by my father's illness.

I exit the greenhouse, secure the padlock, and return home.

Probably best not to bring up the unsecured building. It will only embarrass her if she realizes she forgot something so important. Her greenhouse contains medicinal and ritual herbs. One of the few structures in the North Pole that actually has a lock. It's for the safety of the young elves. They may wander in for fun and get into plants that could cause them harm. When my mother announced that she would lock the structure, she said, "Better safe than sorry," and everyone agreed.

The joy of baking immediately brightens my day. The delicious spices in the gingerbread make my heart tingle in anticipation.

I've grown so used to the cookie cutters in the human world, I'd almost forgotten how I used to cut these shapes freehand. I'm a little out of practice, but still quite proud of my little gingerbread elves and reindeer.

After popping the first tray in the oven, I get to work on the icing. Santa always likes a little extra icing on the side. Like father, like daughter, I suppose.

When the first batch is cool enough to

transfer to a plate, I grab some extra icing and head up to Papa's room. To my delight, he's awake.

"Papa! I made cookies."

He struggles to lift his arm. "Marshmallow! I thought it was one of my fever dreams. How wonderful! You've come home."

"Of course. The children have to have their toys."

His features strain with worry. "Is it that close to Christmas?"

"Yes, Papa. It's only three days away. Are you feeling better?" His eyes may be open, but there's no sparkle, and there's no color in his cheeks.

"Seeing you always makes me feel better, Marshmallow."

Before my adventure in the human world, I never would've noticed the lie. My father is half-human and half-angel. Not a drop of elf. Seems like the human part of him does have the ability to lie. Hmmmm.

I suppose he's simply trying to be brave for me. "Well, these homemade gingerbread cookies are sure to help."

Setting the plate atop the blanket, I adjust it for him. A weak smile pushes up his round cheeks. "Baking really is your gift."

"Thank you, Papa."

He digs into the plate of cookies and polishes them and the extra icing off in no time.

Struggling, he leans toward me.

"What is it, Papa?"

He whispers, "Can you bring me another plate for supper?"

"I can bring as many plates as you want. And I'll definitely bring you more for supper."

Papa pats my hand. His touch is quite cold, and there's no strength in his fingers. Swallowing the emotion threatening to burst from my eyes, I hug him tightly and kiss his cheek. "Now you get some rest. And I promise I'll bring you another plate of cookies when you wake up."

His voice fades as he drifts off, but he murmurs softly, "I got my present early this Christmas."

MAMA RETURNS FROM YOGA to find me powering through a mound of gingerbread cookies. She's not pleased.

"Cynthia! You started your day with a healthy breakfast. Now this?" She gestures toward the plate.

"What can I say, Mama? It's probably the Claus in me that makes me eat so many cookies this time of year." Technically, that is the truth. And I made no mention of what makes me eat so many cookies the rest of the year. Seems like my one-quarter-human side might be gaining a foothold.

She mixes up a concoction and downs it in three large gulps.

Is it possible she's on some crazy diet? "Mama, I wanted to tell you how great you look. Weight really doesn't matter. It's more important that you're healthy. Especially with everything going on with Papa."

The normally stoic elven queen bursts into tears. "I thought I was doing the right thing."

Hopping out of my chair, I hurry over to pat Mama's back. "You're taking care of Papa. Of course you're doing the right thing."

She swipes at her tears and shakes her head. "He may never meet his father."

Her words make no sense. As my brain spins through fruitless attempts to find meaning, a slight movement catches my eye. My mother's right hand slides down to her abdomen.

My mouth goes dry, and my brain refuses to accept the information.

The mechanical patting of my mother's back continues as I struggle to get a grip on reality.

She clears her throat, steps away, and runs a slender finger under each eye. "I should have told you." Her breath catches. "When you left the North Pole, at first your father and I thought it was a phase. Something you'd outgrow. We thought you'd return within a couple of months. When that failed to happen, we discussed alternative plans for succession. It hardly seemed necessary, with your father's unusually long life, but we have a business to run and thousands of elves to think about. Eventually, we landed on the idea of having another child."

My instincts were right, even though I couldn't form the words. My mother is pregnant. My feelings are all over the place. I need to pick one. "I'm going to be a big sister?"

Her wise eyes plead for mercy. "Yes. Are you upset?" Both of her hands cover her abdomen protectively.

"Upset? Why would I be upset? This is wonderful news, Mama. I'm so excited for you and—" The impact of my father's illness hits me like a ton of bricks.

As though my mother can read my mind, she nods slowly and blinks back tears. "We thought we had more time. Time for this little guy to grow up. To ride in Santa's sleigh, as you did when you were a child. But now—"

Reaching out, I place my hand on top of my mother's and smile with all the love in my heart. "Now, I'm here. I'll make sure everything goes smoothly this year, and, between the two of us, we'll get Papa back on his feet. Don't fret, Mama. We'll figure everything out."

The fear in her eyes remains, but she manages a half smile. "I knew we could count on you, Cynthia. You're a good daughter."

"Thank you, Mama."

She hugs me and exhales with a weary grin.

"I made Papa a batch of cookies. He seemed cheerful when I left him. I'm almost certain he'll feel better tomorrow, Mama."

"I'm sure you're right, Cynthia." She wanders off toward the first floor office, and I stare, speechless, at the dirty cup left on the counter. Something is definitely distracting the elven queen. It's more than her pregnancy. Papa's illness is wearing her down.

Rising from the table, I wash my dishes and my mother's cup.

There's not much more I can do here until suppertime. May as well walk down to the bakery and see if I can lend Jelly, Willow, and Violet a hand.

The streets remain quiet, but, as I near the bakery, I see a lone elf scurry out the front door with a platter of cookies.

From this distance, my elf-enhanced sight confirms it's Willow.

Jelly is thrilled to see me. "Cindy! Can't believe I'm seeing you twice in one day."

"Great to see you, too. Looks like you're on your own. I saw Willow leave on a delivery. Did Violet head home early?"

"Oh, never." Jelly puts a hand on her cheek and tilts her head. "Violet works round the clock. She has a little cot in the back. She just had to gather some supplies. I'm sure she'll be back in no time."

"Got it. I'm here to help until then. What can I do?"

Jelly grins enthusiastically. "I'm putting the finishing touches on a batch of focaccia. I've rolled out these four trays. I'm doing two savory and two honey, fig, and goat cheese. Which ones would you like to prepare?"

Falling into my routine of old, I step into the back and grab the largest apron I can find. Tying it snugly around my waist, I return to the prep table and grab the savory trays. Carefully pulling leaves from sprigs of fresh rosemary, I dot them across the focaccia. Then I follow with sun-dried tomatoes, North Pole grown Kalamata olives, and finish with freshly-grated reindeer Parmesan. Now that I have experienced the cow's milk version, I can honestly say I prefer reindeer.

Jelly finishes her sweet offerings and places the four trays in her oversized oven. "Thanks for the help, Cindy. Reminds me of the good old days."

I definitely won't be reminding her they were

only the good old days for her. For me, those were the hardest days of my life. Losing myself in something I loved every day, only to return home and face the looming specter of taking over the family business. Now, here I am.

"Cindy, is everything okay?"

I don't want to burden Jelly with my problems. There's a version of the truth that will work. "Must be tired. That magical travel and a full day at the North Pole have finally caught up with me. I better head home and get a plate of supper cookies up to Papa."

"Makes sense to me. Should we stop our deliveries while you're in town? I'm sure Santa prefers your cookies." Jelly smiles and winks, just like her mother.

"Thanks, but I'll be pretty busy with the toy stuff. You better keep up the deliveries. Papa can't make it without his cookies." We share a giggle, and I place my apron on the counter as I leave.

CHAPTER 7

*H*urrying home under the shimmering glow of the aurora borealis reminds me of the things I truly miss about the North Pole. All is quiet on the first floor, and I wonder if Mama has slipped off to bed early.

Grabbing a clean plate from the cupboard, I pile up some gingerbread cookies and add a side of extra icing. As I approach Papa's room, I hear pleasant voices.

When I knock, he calls me in with a steady voice.

"Papa! You look so much better. How are you feeling?"

"Must be those cookies, Marshmallow." He reaches out both hands and wiggles his fingers.

I place the plate in his hands and pull up a footstool. Mama sits on the end of the bed and her eyes are bright with fresh hope.

"There must be something in those cookies you made, Cynthia. I haven't seen your father this bright eyed in weeks. I knew it was a good idea to bring you home."

That's not a discussion I want to have with my parents. So I focus on the positive. "It would be my pleasure to make dozens of cookies every day, if it helps, Papa."

He wipes gingerbread crumbs from his glorious white mustache and smiles. A hint of rosy color rises in his cheeks.

"I'm going to run downstairs and make peppermint hot chocolate. Can I make some for you, Mama?"

She smiles. "Maybe just this once. We are celebrating."

With a grateful smile, I bob my head and walk downstairs. It doesn't take long for me to whip up three steaming mugs of peppermint hot chocolate. I place extra marshmallows in Papa's cup, and exactly five in Mama's. No sense pushing my luck.

I set the mugs on a small tray and head upstairs.

"Here we go." We each take a mug and lift

them as Mama says, "To Santa and his magnificent sleigh."

After sips of cocoa, Papa wipes his mouth and his expression grows serious. "This will be your first time on the route all by yourself, Marshmallow. Are you sure you can handle it?"

"Papa, if you remember, I'm the one who came up with the new route. I won't let you down. I promise." He smiles and looks at Mama. "Don't forget to give her the sleeping dust . . . and you must have some way to help her get those reindeer in the air."

Mama cradles her mug in two hands and breathes deeply for almost a full minute. "The sleeping dust is easy. You know what to do with that, right, Cynthia?"

"Yes, Mama. If any children are still awake or sneak out of their room, I simply blow a pinch of the sleeping dust and tell them to have wonderful dreams of Santa Claus."

Mama nods with all business. "Correct. Getting a reindeer in the air is a different problem. Something in your father's angelic bloodline connects to these creatures in a way I've been unable to explain. Perhaps we need to make a visit to the stables in the morning for a practice round."

Blizzards! There's nothing worse than me attempting to use magic in front of my mother. I've never had her gifts. The possibility that I may be able to see ghosts came as a shock to all of us. "Yes, Mama. I'll do my best."

"Well, Cynthia, I'm confident I can create some flying powder if our practice session is unsuccessful. However, I feel it would be simpler if you only had to keep track of the sleeping dust. You understand?"

"I do." She's treating me like a fifty-year-old elf. The meaning under her words is clear. Mama's not confident in giving me two different magical powders. She's concerned I'll mix them up and there will be flying children and sleeping reindeer. Cookie crumbs! When will she start treating me like an adult?

"I'm going to turn in. It was a long day, and I want to be at my best tomorrow." Pushing the footstool into the corner, I lean over Santa and softly kiss his forehead. "Sleep well, Papa. I'll bring more cookies in the morning."

He looks up with the eager grin of a child and whispers, "That's my Marshmallow."

"See you in the morning, Mama."

She nods her regal head once, and I softly close the door behind me as I step into the hallway.

When I return to my room, curiosity about the

human world gets the best of me. I pull my magic globe of the entire world down from the top shelf in my closet and place it on my desk. Searching the continents, I locate the Great Lakes and Silver Shoals. When I push my finger against the surface, a bubble, similar to a snow globe, appears. Through this "window" I can observe, without being seen.

Images flicker before my eyes. Cinnamon Roll is hard at work in the bakery. Artikoa paces in front of her like the captain of an army, and there's no one out front. I'm not good at calculating time differences, but it must be either the middle of the night or extra early in the morning. Arti is doing his best to help Cinnamon understand humans.

I want to peer into Keith's apartment, but that feels invasive. Artikoa should arrive tomorrow. Perhaps he'll have an update for me.

Pulling my finger from the magic globe, my heart stutters. It's hard to believe, but that little town I've been exploring for the past two years feels more like home than the North Pole ever has. I'm grateful for my upbringing and my heritage, but earning my independence and making my way is what ignites my passion.

. . .

"**Jingle Bells**" **blasts from the speakers**, and I sit bolt upright in bed, rubbing my eyes and gazing around in confusion. Mama is nowhere to be seen. Perhaps she stayed with Papa.

Dragging my feet from the bed, I head to my closet to see what was left behind. There's a dark blue sweater with gorgeous shimmering gold stars and a pair of matching leggings. That seems like the perfect outfit for today.

Quickly getting dressed, I scrape my hair into a messy ponytail and take a deep breath as I creep downstairs.

The elven queen is hard at work in the kitchen, making a healthy breakfast for everyone.

I give her a quick hug and fill a little plate with cookies. When I reach my father's room, I'm shocked by his appearance. His cheeks are once again ashen, and there is no light in his eyes.

Reaching for the empty plate beside his bed, I note light-colored cookie crumbles and evidence of powdered sugar.

"Papa, did you get up in the night for a snack?"

He nods weakly. "I was feeling better. So I got hungry."

Taking the empty plate, I place the gingerbread cookies beside him. "Were these Linzer cookies? Is that what you ate for your snack?"

He nods. "You know raspberry jam is my weakness."

Softly kissing his cheek, I call over my shoulder as I leave. "Anything with sugar in it is your weakness this time of year, Papa." He attempts to laugh but only utters a raspy cough.

Back downstairs, I set the plate on the counter and turn to my mother. "Did you make these Linzer cookies, Mama?"

"No, dear. I have them delivered from the bakery. With all of my duties this time of year, especially with your father taking ill, I don't have time for baking."

I promised myself I wouldn't mention the unlocked greenhouse, but my amateur sleuth wheels are turning. "I know how busy you are, and I hate to bring this up."

She downs the last of her strange-colored beverage and turns toward me. "What's on your mind, Cynthia?"

"Were you in your greenhouse yesterday, Mama?"

She pauses and her eyes move slowly back and forth as she replays her schedule from yesterday. "No. I didn't have time to visit any of the greenhouses yesterday. Is there a problem?" Mama crosses her arms and lifts her chin.

I hope I'm not about to step in reindeer poop.

"Your private greenhouse was unlocked. I went in to say hi to you, but no one was in there. I secured the door and came home. Are you the only one with a key?"

A flash of guilt washes over her features. An emotion I can't remember ever seeing. "Mama, what's going on?"

She tugs at the tip of her pointed ear and swallows. "I made a key for the elf at the bakery. She's very bright. Willow is working on some new formulas for reindeer shampoo and something else. I'm so distracted these days, I just can't remember."

"Reindeer shampoo? When did we start using that?"

"Oh, the elves at the stables have always had their own methods for cleaning the reindeer, especially before Christmas Eve, but this shampoo sounds like it would make their jobs easier. You know how every minute counts on December 24th."

She glances at the floor and shifts her weight from one foot to the other.

"I understand, Mama. That's thoughtful of you to want to make things easier for the reindeer wranglers. Why does that upset you?"

She presses her delicate fingers to her chest and sighs. "I should have given you a key. My daughter.

The heir to the kingdom. It was wrong of me to keep that from you."

The thought hadn't even occurred to me. Now that she's mentioned it, it does seem odd that she would give this random elf a key to her private greenhouse before her daughter. Oh well. Mama and I have always had an interesting relationship.

"Don't worry about it, Mama. I moved away. You needed help. It's totally understandable. No frosty feelings, I promise."

Her pinched shoulders relax, and she hugs me tight. "I'm so glad you're home, Marshmallow."

Mama never calls me Marshmallow . . . almost never. She's definitely upset. "Are you upset because Papa's doing worse again?"

She blinks back tears as she nods. "He was nearly his old self last night. I can't imagine what happened."

"Mama, after magic practice, will you take me on a tour of your greenhouse?"

She pulls a delicate silver cord from around her neck and reveals a key. Placing her hand underneath it, she taps her fingers twice and a second key appears. Mama hands it to me and smiles wistfully. "I will. And now you have your own key. From now on, there are no secrets between us. No secrets."

Throwing my arms around her, I hug tightly.

"That sounds wonderful. And thank you for the key."

Her hands slide down my arms and grip my elbows. Her brilliant emerald eyes stare deeply into mine. "Perhaps you can tell me about Keith Winters on the tour."

Snowflakes! I should've known there'd be a catch.

CHAPTER 8

*M*other leads the way to the reindeer stable and selects two of her favorites. The great-great-great-granddaughter of Vixen and a recruit from last year who performed so well he earned a spot on the sleigh his first season in the dome. Mama calls him her little Chipmunk, but the sign on his stall simply says "Chip."

The reindeer require no harnesses. My mother's way with animals immediately puts them at ease, and they follow her to the paddock without question.

Without Artikoa to translate, I'm worried we might not be able to get our point across.

Hmmmm, I actually miss that sly little fox. I

never thought I'd feel that way about him. It's strange how the creature I initially thought of as an imposition has become my closest confidant.

"Cynthia, please stand next to Vixen IV and stroke her neck."

Doing as my mother asks, I prepare for the worst.

Vixen does not float off the ground. In fact, her fur doesn't even ruffle. I may as well be making useless snowballs and throwing them at the side of the bright-red stable like I used to do in my early twenties.

Mama steps closer, strokes the cow's neck and whispers softly. Turning to me, she explains. "She understands you're learning, Marshmallow. There's no need to be afraid."

"Okay, but I thought it was your magic that made the reindeer fly."

My mother steps back, and a warm pride floods her viridian eyes. "Oh, Cynthia. It would take a proper incantation worked into each harness, blended with an enormous dose of magic to make it so. The truth is, your father's angel half is what connects to these majestic mammals and gives them wings."

This information shocks me. The bedtime story I've heard hundreds of times says that father and Artikoa negotiated with the reindeer, and father's touch lifted the bull from the ground. As a child, I'd assumed my mother added that embellishment out of her love for my father.

"I never knew. Despite the legend, I believed it was your magic." Twisting my hands, I'm not sure how to tell her how much this new information concerns me. "I'm only one quarter angel. What if I don't have Papa's touch?"

"Nonsense, Cynthia. Even if you only had a drop of angel blood, it wouldn't matter. What matters is belief in yourself. Can you imagine a sleigh full of toys flying around the world, bringing joy to children everywhere? Can you?"

My mother's words touch a dormant piece of my heart. To leave the North Pole and pursue my passion for baking, I had to close off my connection to toys.

The truth is, I love toys! I love presents in general. Who doesn't?

"I think I can, Mama."

"You have to open that part of your heart and remember that first ride on the sleigh with Papa." Her delicate smile curves as she leans toward me.

"Okay, Mama. I'll never forget my first ride on the sleigh. The moon was full, the stars were twinkling like drops of silver magic, and every time Papa delivered a present he would glow a little more. By the time we got back to the

North Pole, he was brighter than Rudolph's nose!"

She grips both my shoulders and rubs them encouragingly. "Yes! That's it. Remember each of those moments as though they were happening right now, and then touch Vixen's neck."

I sink into the memory. It feels as though it's happening all over again. Reaching out, I stroke Vixen's neck. I still have my eyes squeezed shut, but my mother's gasp forces them open.

The reindeer's fur stands on end as though she's carrying a charge of static electricity!

"Okay. Keep going, darling. Remember how you felt. Shift the focus from Santa to yourself. How did you feel planning the perfect Christmas gift delivery route?"

As my heart fills with joy, tingles travel outward through my arms and legs.

This time when I touch the reindeer's fur, she lifts almost a foot in the air.

When my mother squeezes my arm, I lose my focus and the deer clatters to the snow. Mama quickly apologizes to the patient reindeer and asks her to return to the stable. "You're next."

The large male reindeer steps forward and nuzzles the queen's shoulder as though he were an arctic fox kit.

Queen Erregina coaches me through the visualization and stresses the importance of feeling my feelings. Not just imagining things.

I close my eyes tight. Crisp night air whooshes by as I sit on a shiny red sleigh. The huge moon feels close enough to touch . . .

"Marshmallow! Look!"

Hesitantly opening my eyes, I'm shocked to see Chip floating several feet above my head.

"How do I get him down — safely?"

Mama hugs an arm around my shoulders. "Easy. Imagine it to be as you wish — and it is so."

I picture the gentle descent of the reindeer, and his hooves softly pressing into the fluffy white snow. Then I watch in amazement as my thoughts become reality.

Mama squeezes my hand, and the three of us walk back to the stable. She gives Vixen IV and Chip each an extra carrot before we leave the stable in search of greenhouses.

On the way to the farm, our nickname for the greenhouses, my mother sings my praises. In my 117 years, I've never been paid this many compliments. If I totaled up all the compliments my mother has paid me in my lifetime, it wouldn't be this many.

"Cynthia, your papa will be so proud. With the power of Christmas Eve on your side and a sleigh full of presents, you'll have no trouble. You really are amazing. It seems you're the best parts of your father and me. How fortunate."

"Thanks, Mama. It'll be fun to help out. Papa will be feeling better in no time. But it's no problem to take care of things this year." My left hand squeezes my right, as my thoughts spin through unwelcome possibilities.

Mother stops, grips one of my hands, and turns me toward her. "What? You've taken the reins. Why would you want your father to take them back?"

Now this is the mother I remember from my youth. I have no intention of getting into an argument after we enjoyed such a wonderful time. It's best for me to focus on something else.

"I'm definitely looking forward to seeing your garden. You have such a way with nature."

She hesitates for a moment before walking onward. Since our lovely magic lesson, we're both reluctant to upset the sleigh, if you will.

Passing between two large greenhouses, we approach the door of my mother's private bio-dome.

As I wait for her to open the lock, she turns and smiles. "Why not use your key? A little celebration."

"Oh, of course!"

Slipping the key from my pocket, I unlock the door and follow my mother into her home away from home. The temperature is quite cozy, and the humidity is heavy. Suddenly, I'm wishing I'd worn short sleeves.

Mama walks down each row, talking about heirloom seeds, the importance of cross-pollination, and the precious bee colonies she oversees.

"Cynthia, you seem distracted."

"Sorry, Mama. I'm trying to listen, but it's so hot in here."

My mother blinks several times and her chin juts out. "The temperature is ideal for the proper propagation of these many species. I'm sure you would—" Her speech ends abruptly as she walks toward a fascinating vine bearing speckled bean-like fruits.

"Is something wrong?"

She turns. "The soil is disturbed here. I must've brushed my trowel across when I was moving past this to the black Valentine beans." She bites her bottom lip. "Yes. That must be what happened."

Reaching toward the intriguing vine between Mama and the black Valentine plant, I snap off a bean and move to pop it into my mouth. My mother grabs my hand, almost violently, and commands, "No. Drop that."

Dropping the bean in the dirt, I shrink away from the powerful queen. "You always let me sample from your garden. What did I do?"

"The reason we lock this greenhouse, Cynthia, is because not everything is safe to eat. That particular bean is not edible. Castor beans are used to produce turkey-red oil, which is an important ingredient in shampoo. Remember when I mentioned we're developing a new cleanser for the reindeer as well."

"Oh, sorry. I forgot."

My mother swirls her finger over the bean and it vanishes from existence. "Not to worry, Cynthia. But now that you have a key, you must be extra careful if you enter the premises alone."

"How will I know what's safe and what isn't?"

My mother gives me a quick rundown of the map near the front door of the greenhouse. The contents are divided into sections by colors of the rainbow. Those plants in the red sector are nonedible. Small descriptions and instructions follow each color on the chart.

"Thank you, Mama. That's very helpful, and I'm glad there's a cheat sheet. I seem to have no trouble remembering ingredients for my recipes, but I'm sure this information would have escaped me as soon as I walked out. Thanks again for the tour."

A flash of irritation touches her eyes at the mention of my recipes, but she remains silent.

It appears I'm going to skate through this

without having to talk about Keith. A smile lifts the corner of my mouth.

Mother locks the greenhouse and takes my hand as we walk home. "Now tell me about Keith Winters."

Blizzards!

CHAPTER 9

*A*s Mama and I wind our way home, she stops abruptly and clutches her amulet. I can see a glow creeping between her fingers.

"What is it?"

She closes her eyes, and a whisper escapes her lips. "Artikoa."

In a flash, my father's most trusted advisor and my undercover sidekick in the human world, Artikoa, stands beside us.

Without thinking, I fall to one knee and throw my arms around his neck. "Arti! I missed you. How's everything in Silver Shoals?"

My mother's left hand still clutches at her amulet, and her chin drops like saltwater taffy left too long on the hook.

Realizing my terrible faux pas, I swallow, clear my throat twice, and get to my feet. "Most Venerable Elder, what is your report?"

My mother's shock remains, while Artikoa recovers nicely. "It is good to see you as well, Cynthia. Silver Shoals is much as you left it. We had a brief snowstorm, but the plows were on it within the hour. You would be quite pleased with Cinnamon Roll's progress. She is keeping up production and has learned much of the human slang. As expected, our queen made the right choice."

"That's great news." Having just finished an uncomfortable discussion about Keith Winters, I hesitate to reopen that subject, but curiosity gets the best of me. "Did you remember to say goodbye to Keith for me?"

Arti sinks back onto his haunches, and a smug grin appears to soften his pointed snout. "As you know, Cynthia, I'm unable to speak English to humans. However, Cinnamon Roll passed along your farewell and embellished heavily."

What started as good news has suddenly turned terrifying. "What do you mean, *embellished?*"

The sly fox's nearly invisible eyebrows lift. "Oh, she said you were terribly sorry you had to leave without a proper goodbye and that you'd be thinking of him on your travels. I believe she also mentioned something about looking forward to a welcome home kiss."

For a split second, the color drains from my face, then an intense heat rushes up from my stomach, turning my Claus cheeks an intense rosy glow.

Mother, at last regaining her composure, crosses her arms and tilts her head. "A welcome home kiss, is it? The topic of Mr. Winters needs to be revisited."

"I promise it doesn't. I promise everyone — it doesn't. Let's get inside and discuss tomorrow's schedule. I have a lot to accomplish, and I haven't done most of it before."

Artikoa appears to puff his fur with extra drama as he leads our procession indoors.

Mama prepares dinner, while Arti and I head up to Papa's room.

When I open the door, Artikoa inhales sharply and comes to a standstill. "It is worse than I feared."

Surging forward, I glance at the plate beside my father's bed. More cookie crumbs. Definitely not gingerbread.

"He won't stop eating those cookies."

Papa's most trusted advisor twists his head sideways in confusion. "This time of year, he seldom eats anything else."

"Well, they're making him sick. It's too much

sugar. If Papa was at his best, it would have no effect. But since he's already under the weather . . ."

"What of your mother's healing potions? Any success there?"

"I don't think she's tried anything different since I arrived. She mentioned she had tried different combinations before I came home, and had no results. The only thing that seemed to make him better were my gingerbread cookies."

Artikoa shakes his head. "Don't be too full of yourself, Cynthia. Cookies are cookies. If your belief is that sugar is not beneficial in his current state, gingerbread cookie sugar would have much the same effect as Linzer cookie sugar."

My shoulders fall. "I suppose you're right."

He sniffs the air and motions with his nose for me to follow him from the room. As we descend the staircase, he continues the discussion. "I'm able to smell if your father's blood sugar is too high. There was no such odor in the room. Whatever is sapping his strength, I don't believe it to be sugar related."

At the dinner table, Mama sits in relative silence as Artikoa and I go over the lengthy checklist for Christmas Eve.

"Have you met the reindeer?"

"Yes. They seem cheerful to be working with me. Or at least not upset." I shrug.

He turns to my mother. "Has she been able to achieve lift off?"

My mother briefly recaps the magic lesson and assures the arctic fox that, with the additional magic of Christmas Eve, all will be well.

"Everything seems in order. That simply leaves her suit."

"My what?"

His sharp nose lifts. "You can hardly slide down chimneys and magic yourself into the living rooms of children all over the world dressed in your usual attire, Cynthia. You must have a suit. And we'll have to create some kind of wig to cover that bright red hair."

"You've got to be kidding! Why stop there?" Now for a dash of that sarcasm humans adore. "Why not give me a fake beard and mustache, too?"

"Excellent idea. I shall discuss it with the elves at once."

My attempt at sarcasm fails miserably, and, before I can protest, Artikoa glides from his chair and vanishes from the room. Why did I have to mention the beard? I can't begin to imagine how annoying it will be flying around in the sleigh all night with a fake beard scratching my face!

Melting snowballs! How do I get myself into these things?

Mother announces she's turning in early, leaving me alone at the kitchen table.

Getting to my feet, I toy with the idea of baking, but Artikoa rushes into the room with a hint of a grin. "That was easier than I imagined. Have a seat, Cindy."

I don't have the energy to argue. I fall into a chair and rest my elbows on the table.

Arti takes this opportunity to quiz me on gift delivery protocol. "What is the protocol if there is no chimney?"

"Magic myself to the Christmas tree. Wherever they've chosen to place it. Deliver the presents and place candy canes in the stockings, if they've hung them in their home."

Crossing my arms, I tilt my head and silently dare him to stump me.

"What about the cookies and milk?"

"I eat them, of course!"

"Incorrect. You examine the milk to make sure it is not an alcoholic beverage, and you carefully look over the cookies for any obvious signs of tampering."

"What?"

He exhales. "You and I both know there are a significant number of humans on the Naughty List. Naughty List and Nice List humans are known to cohabitate. The last thing we need is an intoxicated Santa, or one that falls prey to a cookie laced with some type of sedative. We need you at your best for the entire route. Understood?"

I open and close my mouth twice, searching for a response I can't seem to find. The thought of anyone purposefully interfering with Santa's ability to deliver presents had never occurred to me. My heart hurts as I think about the possibility. "Sounds terrible. I'll just toss the cookies in the present bag. I'm not taking any chances."

I half expect him to protest. Artikoa nods in agreement. "That would be best. Especially with your father's current situation."

"What do you mean, his current situation?"

"We cannot rule out foul play." A ripple of concern ruffles the fur on Arti's back. "You focus on your Christmas Eve duties, and I'll look into matters here at the Pole. Perhaps we will truly have a gift to give your mother on Christmas Day."

"You think— Are you saying— You think someone did this to Papa on purpose?"

The wise amber eyes stare at me as though they can read a page from my soul. "I would think your time in the human world would've caused you to make a list of your own."

The words hit home. I had suspected foul play, and I'd pushed the idea away. There's no time to think about that now. I have to get the gifts delivered. I have to make Papa proud. "Okay. I'll go see the tailor tomorrow and get the suit finished."

Visions of Wacky Winkle dance in my healing head. "You might want to start your investigation with Ash, of the forest clan."

Arti tilts his head with interest. "Go on."

"Mr. Winkle said Ash is trying to get the forest clan to leave the North Pole. Oh, and there was a group protesting in front of the factory."

"This is most concerning. Have you informed your mother?"

Shaking my head, I blink back tears. "She's pregnant. I—"

"I sensed as much. Leave it to me."

"When I get back from toy delivery, we can review your findings at the bakery."

"Why the bakery?" Artikoa pinches his small pointed ears together.

"I thought it would be best to talk about it somewhere out of mother's earshot. She's convinced the illness is because of Papa's advanced age. Mama is trying so hard to be brave. If she thought someone—" Emotion steals my voice.

In uncharacteristic fashion, Arti leaps from his chair, strides across the kitchen, and rubs his shoulder against my leg as he takes a seat beside me. "She's not the only one who is being brave, Cynthia. Your father would be very proud of you."

"Thanks. I better get some sleep. I have a pretty big day ahead of me tomorrow."

He nods once and follows me to the foot of the stairs. "I have some things to check on with the starlight crew at the factory. I'll see you for breakfast in the morning, Your Highness."

Crouching beside him, I stroke the soft fur of his cheek smile. "No need for formalities. I'm grateful for all of your help, *MVE*."

He saunters off with a soft chuckle at my shortened version of Most Venerable Elder.

We've become almost-friends. Two years ago, I never would have believed it was possible. Maybe it's the magic of the North Pole, or maybe I'm finally growing up, but I have to admit my father's wisdom in pairing us up was truly remarkable.

Blowing a soft kiss toward Papa's door as I turn down the hallway leading to my wing of our home, I feel that tightness in my chest once more.

If something unsavory is afoot, Arti and I will figure it out.

CHAPTER 10

When I push open my bedroom door, I'm surprised to find Mama and Artikoa deep in a serious debate. Mama sits with both hands on her barely rounded belly. "Not all the elves are cheerful about our news. The forest clan is especially displeased with the plans to hand over the reins to a new heir."

"All the elves are loyal to Santa. Why would there be any hint of disagreement about maintaining the operation?" Artikoa sits proudly on a red-velvet ottoman.

"When we — when I met St. Nicholas — I was protecting seven different clans of elves. We had united against our common enemy, the barbarian tribe from the East. The elven clans all agreed to relocate, and for centuries they were overjoyed making toys and living under my protection in the dome."

"Yes. Everyone is well looked after. Santa is good to them." Arti's tail curls around his feet.

A twinge of hurt tightens the muscles in my mother's jaw. "We're both good to them. After centuries of peace, they've grown complacent. Some of the elves who carried the lore have passed, most recently the gentle Sequoia. The oral tradition continues, but, without the first-hand experiences of fighting the barbarians, these younger generations have lost their fear of the outside world."

I'd love to tell her that there's more to celebrate than to fear, but I'm one of the younger generation. Best to keep my mouth closed at this point. Maybe I'll learn something from their debate.

"Do you suspect an uprising?" Artikoa is on his feet. His gaze narrows.

"There have been rumblings." The queen sighs and wags her head in dismay. "The forest clan has the youngest elder of all, Ash, Sequoia's son. He's a mere 317. That's far too young to guide such a large contingent of elves. They have strength in numbers, Artikoa. If they move against me — I may have to open the dome and release nearly one quarter of our population."

Surprised by Mama's knowledge of Ash and the "rumblings," I can no longer maintain my silence. "Mama, what about the toy factory? How can we—"

"Yes, Cynthia, your father's terrible illness isn't the only crisis I'm handling." She crosses her arms firmly over her chest. "We would have to do away with vacations. The factory would be forced to run year round. Our normal shutdown in July would be canceled. We could barely get by." She wipes a shaking hand across her face. "If the forest clan secedes, I fear it's the beginning of the end."

"I had no idea, Mama. We have to get Papa healthy as soon as possible. His passion for toys and Christmas is the only thing that can turn this around."

My mother's slender shoulders sag, and her hands once again cup her belly. "We need more time, Marshmallow. Your brother needs time to grow up, learn the business, and practice his magic."

An inner voice warns that this conversation might be taking a dangerous turn. It would be quite easy for my brilliant mother to manipulate me into making promises I don't want to keep. Best to steer away from that.

"Are there any elves in the forest clan that would do this? Do something to Papa?" Artikoa tilts his head in response to my comment. His look is a mix of agreement and worry.

Pure shock erases every other emotion from Mama's face. "Attack Santa? No. No, they would never—" Her outburst is adamant at the start, but it quickly fizzles.

"I would hate to think it, too, Mama. People do strange things when they're under enough stress."

Her hands fly to her hips, and defensive anger flickers in her eyes. "People, yes. One of the reasons we were so against you leaving the dome, Cynthia. *People* do horrible things! Not elves. Elves are not vengeful."

My time among humans may have tipped the scales in their favor in my mind. I feel as protective of my kindhearted human friends as my mother does of the life growing inside of her.

"What about the barbarian wars, Mama? Are you telling me that elves fought against the barbarians with kindness and love? Impossible. Elves are capable of heinous acts. Maybe they justified it with the need to protect their clans, but how is that any different from what might be happening right now? Someone in the forest elf clan may believe strongly enough in the protests and convictions of Ash to force your hand. If there is no Santa, then there is no Christmas."

The defensive anger fizzles out, and my mother runs from the room in tears.

Crashing glaciers! We're no closer to figuring out what's wrong with Papa, and now I've insulted my mother's entire race.

"That was unduly harsh, Cynthia." Arti shakes his head.

"She has to face the truth. I didn't mean to upset her, but — I may as well head down to the bakery."

He leaps from his perch, intending to follow.

"I'll see you in the morning, Arti."

"If you do not return in one hour, I will hunt you down."

"Yes, Most Venerable Elder."

Racing from the house, I scrape my hair into a messy bun and twist one of my worn out scrunchies around and around. Time to stuff my face with anything I can get my hands on.

When I enter the bakery, Willow is manning the counter.

She lowers her gaze and steps back from the counter.

"Hello, Willow. What's good tonight?"

"The Linzer cookies are fresh, Your Highness."

Leaning my elbows on the counter, I look down at the selection of pastries. "Please call me

Cindy. I'll take a cinnamon roll and two ginger-bread cookies. With extra icing, please."

Willow curtsies, avoids eye contact, and loads a plate with my selections. She pushes it across the counter and steps back.

"Where's Jelly?"

Her gaze darts to the corner. "She's — she's sleeping in the back."

What a weird reaction. Not sure why my presence makes Willow so uncomfortable, but I certainly don't mind if Jelly takes a nap. Who would? Oh, maybe Mama, I suppose. "It's great that you're handling everything. Jelly and Violet are lucky to have you."

She nods once, but remains silent.

A sudden thought tickles my brain. "Willow, are you from the forest clan?"

The diminutive elf bites her bottom lip and wrings her hands. "Yes."

Her voice goes up at the end, almost as though she's asking a question.

"Are you sure?" I give a soft chuckle to let her know I'm being friendly, but Willow stiffens.

She gestures to the back room. "I should check on Jelly."

"Okay. Tell Jelly I said 'hi.'"

Willow scurries into the back as though I've shouted at her.

Taking my treats to go, I wander out of the shop and head toward the community square.

On Christmas Day, after I return from *hopefully* delivering all the presents with success, this area will spill over with celebrating elves. There will be food of all kinds, our massive tree will light up, and handmade ornaments with the names of all the elves born this year will be added to the tree. Finishing my last gingerbread cookie, I lick the icing from my fingers as I walk toward the ancient pine brought from Europe during the relocation.

Starting at due north, I walk five steps east and count seven rows of branches up.

There, on a branch decorated with holly leaves and cranberries, is a tiny red sleigh with gold lettering: Cynthia Cherubim Claus.

Mother told me the entire village cheered when she placed my ornament on the tree. It's just like her to lead the community celebration less than twelve hours after giving birth. True, elves heal much more quickly than humans, but, to this day, I believe Mama used quite a bit of magic to prop herself up that day.

Returning to my bench, I gaze at the tree with sadness and a hint of worry. Will my brother bring the clans together? Or will the North Pole vanish into myth and legend? So few humans believe in my father as it is. Perhaps that's what is making him sick? The world is losing their sense of wonder, their ability to believe in something good and wholesome.

Blowing a kiss to the beautiful tree, I pick up my empty plate and walk to the bakery to return it. This time, when I open the door, Jelly is leaning on the counter looking more tired than rested.

"Bringing back my plate, Jelly."

She rubs her bleary eyes as she yawns. "Your plate? When were you here?"

"Didn't Willow tell you I said hello?"

"Willow? She's not here. She and Violet had to get some supplies from the greenhouses for me. Where was I?"

"Willow said you were in the back, taking a nap."

Jelly places a hand on her belly and chuckles with all the jolliness of a true elf. "Cookie crumbs! This season is wearing me out! Can't remember what day it is, let alone the last time I took a nap. She probably gave me your message, and I already forgot. What can I get you?"

Wiggling the empty plate, I attempt a comforting smile. "You definitely need some rest, Jelly. I already had my treats. Would you like me to take over for an hour or two so you can get some actual rest?"

"Nonsense. I'll eat a few of these extra fudgy

brownies and I'll be good as new. You have enough on your plate, Cindy."

Our eyes fall to the empty plate, and we share a hearty chuckle.

"Promise me you'll get some rest tonight, Jelly."

She rubs her hands on her apron and smiles. "I promise, Cindy."

Chuckling under my breath, I walk out of the bakery.

It's time to head home and face the Christmas carols.

CHAPTER 11

I'm out of bed before the first carol crackles from the speakers. Despite my exit from the North Pole to open a bakery, I can't deny the thrill of Christmas Eve under the dome.

I'm clearly not alone. Mother and Artikoa are already seated at the breakfast table and glance up in anticipation, despite Papa's illness.

"I'm going to head straight to the tailor's. He's got his work cut out for him making a suit before I have to load the sleigh."

They both nod, and Arti adds, "Grandmother Peony has generously offered her glorious white hair for a wig and beard. Her three daughters and four granddaughters have been working around the clock since I put in the request. I'll fetch the disguise and join you at the tailor's."

Mother glances up at me with a wistful smile. "Why don't you stop at the bakery and have some gingerbread cookies for breakfast, Marshmallow?"

My eyes must be as wide as saucers, because my mother blushes as she chuckles. "I can tell you're surprised. If you're going to do your father's job, you may as well have your father's breakfast."

"Thank you, Mama. Sounds delicious."

If I stick around, I'll say something I'll regret. Turning, I rush from the room faster than a child checking under the tree on Christmas morning.

The streets are buzzing with activity. The normally uncrowded streets are nearly shop-to-shop with excited elves. Each happier than the last. This is the most important day of the year at the North Pole. All the hard work, planning, and extra shifts pay off in the glorious moment Santa and his sleigh take to the skies.

A sudden lump forms in my stomach. I absolutely don't want to disappoint them.

Rushing into the bakery, my eyes light up the moment I see Jelly. "Merry Christmas! I'd like three gingerbread cookies and a side of extra icing, please."

She grabs a gingham-checked plate, piles it with at least five cookies, and two sugar cookie cups filled with extra icing. "Here you go, stand-in Santa!"

Taking a seat at the counter, I dive in to the plate of still-warm gingerbread. "This is the best batch ever!" Suddenly realizing my mistake, I attempt to shovel snow over my tracks. "Oops. Don't tell your mother I said that. Cinnamon Roll makes the best gingerbread cookies. You just whipped up her recipe."

Jelly lifts her small pudgy hands in the air and shakes her head. "I can't take the credit for these. Violet is really coming into her own. She was up all night making extra cookies for today's adventures. She just pulled this batch out of the oven and said they were especially for you, if you came by this morning."

On my third cookie, I carefully swallow and reply, "Cheers to her! This is exactly the breakfast I need to get me going. I'll take these two to go. I have to see Thimble about my suit."

Jelly takes the empty plate and winks. "Lean your ear this way." When I angle across the counter, she whispers a North Pole blessing. "May the stars shine brightly on your sleigh."

"And yours." Tucking the cookies safely in the pocket of my Christmas tree hoodie, I practically skip down the street to the tailor's.

When I step into the shop, Thimble peers

around the heavy brocade curtain and hurries from the back room with a huge smile on his face.

"Miss Claus! Your Highness! I was hoping you would stop by bright and early." He gestures for me to follow. "Right this way. I've basted everything together and created a pillow for you to strap over your stomach. You have a long way to go in the bowl-full-of-jelly department."

Pressing a hand to my stomach, quick tears flash to my eyes, and I send a silent wish into the universe. Papa, please be okay. Please be okay.

Wiping the tears before Thimble can make a fuss, I stride into the back room and stare at the fake belly.

Thimble's son, Tassel, emerges from the stockroom, and his pale-green eyes light up like shimmering gemstones. "Cindy!" He points at the huge belly pillow and snickers. "Looks like all those gingerbread cookies finally caught up with you."

After a short hug and a long laugh, I turn to Thimble to explain.

"Your son once bet me I couldn't eat twenty-five gingerbread cookies in one minute."

The tailor feigns shock. "How did he fare, Your Highness?"

A playful grin touches my cheeks. "Do you remember that time he had to work double shifts at the greenhouses?"

Thimble's mouth gently falls open as he accesses the memory. "Tassel!"

"Oh, come on, Dad." Tassel blushes.

"A thousand apologies, Your Highness." The rosy color drains from Thimble's round cheeks.

"Nonsense, Thimble. It was all in fun. Tassel was one of my best friends." The thought of how we've drifted apart brings a tinge of sadness to my heart. "Tassel, I—"

He picks up the padded belly and shrugs. "We'll always be friends, Cindy. Time and distance won't change that." His cheeks redden as he steps toward me.

Uh oh. Perhaps Tassel wants to be more than friends. My time in the human world has opened my eyes to unspoken emotions. Best keep things light.

"That's great, Tass. Will you help me get that contraption on?"

He avoids my gaze and offers a bow of his head.

When I step onto the platform, Thimble drapes the fabric of a half-sewn jacket and trousers around my body as his fingers fly from pincushion to velvet.

In less than ten minutes, he has everything pinned to fit me perfectly.

Glancing into the gilded mirror, my heart

nearly breaks in two. Aside from the fiery red hair, I'm the spitten image of my father.

Thimble steps back, takes a straight pin from his teeth, and smiles proudly. "Once we get Peony's wig on that head of yours, there won't be a child in all of Christmas who will know you're a stand-in. Santa would be most proud, Your Highness."

"Thank you. I don't want to disappoint the children." Stepping carefully from the platform, I smile down at the skilled tailor and his son. "Can you two help me out of this thing? I'm due at the stables."

In practiced fashion, their fingers fly to remove the suit and transfer it to the dress form in a flash. "I should have this ready by lunchtime, Your Highness." Thimble bows.

Glancing at the near mountain of pins pushed through the velvet fabric, I take a deep breath. "You are a marvel, Thimble. I'll swing by and pick it up later. The Claus family is eternally grateful."

He waves away my gratitude. "Nonsense. I do this for a love of sewing. No thanks necessary."

Departing the tailor's with a wave to Tassel, I pass the factory and head directly to the stables.

This time, the reindeer wranglers have not been caught unawares. The harnesses are all polished to a shimmering red gleam and the silver bells shine so brightly they appear to glow from within.

"The harnesses look amazing, Zig and Zag! What's the lineup for tonight's ride?"

The twins fold their polishing rags in unison and approach. "Your Highness, we have chosen eight of our veteran reindeer and the newcomer whom you met on your previous visit."

I'm growing accustomed to their duet, but there's a part of me that's unnerved by them speaking in unison. "Wonderful. I'd like to meet each of them. And, if it's not *too* much trouble, can I have one more look at the new recruits?"

"Of course, Your Highness." One bows, one curtsies. They both turn and lead the way into the stables.

There's a level of energy within the stable that feels contagious. Even the reindeer are excited about tonight's journey.

The veterans have a deep sense of calm underneath their excitement. They realize what will be expected of them and they're saving their energy for what's important.

Chipmunk, on the other hand, is all prancing and leaping.

Reaching a hand over the half-door, I rub my fingers together and cluck my tongue.

Chip approaches and presses his nose into my

TRIXIE SILVERTALE

hand. "Sorry, buddy, I should've brought you something." I glance over my shoulder at the twins. "Do either of you have a treat for Chip?"

They exchange a glance that clearly says I've gone off script again, but soon they each produce small apples, and I take them both.

Chip gobbles up the fruit, leans down, and allows me to stroke his head between his large ears. The male reindeer have already lost their antlers for the season, so Santa's team usually consists of more female reindeer than male. "Save your energy. I'm excited too. If we use up all of that excitement before we're in the air, we'll never finish the route. I'm counting on you, Chip. You understand?"

His large trusting eyes seem to settle. I wouldn't believe it if I hadn't seen it myself, but he appears to nod his head.

"I'll see you in a few hours, boy."

Turning to the nervous twins, I attempt a positive tone. "Come on. Let's see those new recruits. I want to give my father a full report."

Zig and Zag stiffen. "A full report. We weren't made aware."

Cookie crumbs! I've done it again. I have to stop mentioning Santa. "Don't worry. It's not official. Just me making sure Santa stays in the loop."

Despite my reassurances, the twins seem

102

stricken. They practically trip over one another as they lead me to the paddock.

"The new recruits always have exercise time in the morning, Your Highness," they chorus.

Glancing across the snowy field, I count nine young reindeer. "I don't want to upset either of you, but, on my first visit, you told me there were ten new recruits. I only count nine. Are you sure there wasn't a miscount?"

Zig and Zag seem to freeze with fear. Their faces pale simultaneously, and I've left them speechless.

Moving to the left, I'm about to count the reindeer a second time when Artikoa bounds through the stable and into the paddock beside me. "Your mother wishes to speak with you — it seems urgent."

"It'll keep." I don't want to lose my train of thought. "Something is not right here." Pointing to the pen, I ask, "Arti, your senses are far more keen than mine. How many reindeer do you see in the paddock?"

Taking only a moment, his predator-based senses survey the scene. "Nine, Your Highness."

Nodding, I snap my fingers. "That's what I thought, too. Zig and Zag assured me that ten new recruits came through the door. Even though my father would've supervised the opening of the door to our sacred dome, in his current condition he may not remember the count. Can you speak to the reindeer? Ask them how many came through?"

Without response, Arti cautiously approaches the herd. Regardless of his status as Most Venerable Elder, and his ability to speak the language of all animals, young reindeer still perceive him as a potential threat.

Two of the smaller beasts run toward the fence line.

Artikoa speaks in a calm tone, and two of the larger bulls approach.

They appear to exchange formalities, and the wise fox poses his question.

After a brief discussion, he thanks them with a gentle bow of his head and returns to me.

"The bulls assure me ten passed through the gate. The smaller one, with a slight limp in his left foreleg, said the tenth reindeer had vanished by morning."

"Vanished? No one can vanish at the North Pole, save perhaps my mother. What does he mean, vanished?"

Artikoa's amber eyes are filled with concern. "I asked the same question, Your Highness. He assures me ten passed through the door. Only nine remain. The other bull who spoke to me, the one missing a tuft of fur near his left ear, mentioned that the tenth reindeer smelled different. They both used the term 'off somehow.' When pressed for details, they were unable to provide them."

Momentarily distracted by the amount of detail Artikoa picked up during his casual chat with the two deer, I struggle to focus. "Artikoa, I have too much to handle today. I need to visit my father and provide him with some assurances. Some . . . good news. Please look into this matter of the recruits?"

"Of course. You focus on delivering those presents. If something is amiss, I will investigate. You and I will enjoy a lovely repast on Christmas Day. Perhaps we will each have good news for the other."

"Here's hoping, Arti. Here's hoping."

Leaving him to wrap things up with the twins, I walk to the factory, patting the two cookies in my pocket. As I think about eating a fourth, my stomach twists. Twitching elf ears! There's my anxiety kicking in. I fully expected it. But I thought my stomach would hold off until we were in the air. Oh well, I can handle it. I've done it before. I nearly lost my cookies when I had to give my first speech at the factory.

Memories rush back, and I can picture a scrawny fifty-three-year-old elf standing at the podium next to Papa. That moment when he stepped away and gestured for me to speak, my stomach felt as though it literally had tied itself in a knot.

The only thing I can do now is take a deep breath and push on. Children of the world are counting on me. They're counting on stand-in Santa.

CHAPTER 12

The twins must have sent word. Anise greets me at the door and takes me directly to the room I've grown up calling "the arena." Hundreds upon hundreds of elves have gathered. As she walks me up the steps, a surge of courage rushes through me. I'm not the same elf who left the North Pole two years ago. I've experienced all kinds of amazing and heartbreaking things in the human world. I can use my experiences to motivate these elves. To give them an idea of what their efforts truly mean.

Anise steps up to the podium. "Good elves, please give Cynthia Claus your attention." She motions for quiet. The applause and cheers subside and all pointed ears tilt my way.

"Merry Christmas, good elves."

The entire crowd responds with a gentle roar. "Merry Christmas."

"I know how hard you've worked this past year, and Santa is extremely proud. Sorry to report he's under the weather, but he knows he can count on all of you."

There are sporadic smiles and concerned murmurs. "I want to tell you that you can count on me. I may have been absent from our lovely home for the last two years, but my experiences in the human world have given me amazing insights."

Taking a moment to catch my breath, I allow my heart to guide me. "Humans are more fragile than any of us realized. They deal with tragedy and death as part of their daily lives. Despite these obstacles, they continue to pick themselves up. Continue to get up every day and take care of their families. This single day out of the year, they count on us to share the burden. I promise you, with your help, we won't let them down. We'll make sure that every child has a gift under the tree. The magic of Christmas will continue." Wild applause erupts from the crowd. My anxiety vanishes in the face of such unconditional support.

"Good elves, the world is counting on us. Load those presents, harness the reindeer, and take to the skies!"

A wave of cheers ripples through the crowd.

Anise steps forward with a mix of awe and admiration in her gentle indigo eyes. Tilting the microphone down, she calls out, "You heard Santa. Stations everyone! This is not a drill. Let the Christmas Eve festivities begin!"

The elves cheer themselves senseless as they rush toward their various assignments. In less than three minutes, the arena is clear. Not a trace of elf remains.

Anise offers a deep curtsy. "Your Highness, that was an inspiring speech. We elves love making toys, but I feel we lose sight of the true meaning of our gifts. You brought the reasons into sharp focus. Thank you." She offers a second curtsy.

Placing a hand on her shoulder, I gaze down with love. "Thank you. You've done an amazing job running the factory this past year. My father will be elated to hear how efficiently you and your many crews met all the deadlines and goals."

A light blush touches her cheeks, and she leads me from the stage to the loading area.

Teams of elves from each division of the factory supervise loading packages into Santa's magic bag.

On the outside, the pine-green velvet bag appears approximately three-feet wide by four- or five-feet tall. However, every present for every child fits in that bag. Mama explained the magic to me when I was a wee elf, but it never made sense. All I know is that everything fits, and when he reaches in Santa gets exactly what he needs, and, with the addition of the perfect route, Christmas remains the most magical day of the year in the human world.

After shaking hands with the team leaders from each division, patting a few backs, and peering into the magical bag, I head back to see Thimble.

If he's kept his word, my suit should be ready. When I arrive, Artikoa waits outside the door with a small bag clutched between his teeth.

Removing the bag, I lean down and whisper, "Have you found anything?"

"My investigation will begin in earnest once you are in the air. For now, we must all focus on the task at hand." He tips his sharp nose toward the bag. "Grandmother Peony and her matrilineal stitchers send their best."

"Thank you, Arti." Opening the door, we both enter as Thimble rushes from the back room.

"Miss Claus! You are exactly on time. To be expected. Please, join me in the back room for your final fitting." He glances at the bag in my hand. "Is that the wig?"

He lunges forward, snatches the bag from my

hand, and gestures manically for the two of us to follow him.

In the back room, there's no sign of Tassel. I strap the pillow over my stomach, slip into the gorgeous velvet suit, and pull on the fake wig and beard.

Artikoa gasps. "If I didn't know better, I'd swear it was Father Christmas himself."

Thimble drops his gaze and whispers, "Thank you."

"You're a miracle worker, Thimble." Turning back and forth, gazing at my reflection, I eventually notice my stockinged feet. "What about the boots?"

Thimble shrugs his narrow shoulders. "Miss Claus, I am a simple tailor. I have no skills as a cobbler. I'm sure if you speak to Thumbtack, he could whip something together."

Arti shakes his head. "You will wear your father's. It is tradition. On a special occasion such as this, we would be foolish to upset tradition."

Thimble carefully assists in the removal of my wardrobe. He packages everything in a glorious garment bag, and quickly adds a special pocket for the wig, beard, and mustache.

Artikoa leads me home. Mama greets us with fresh tears on her flawless cheeks. "Cynthia, what took you so long? He's worse. So much worse."

Leading the trio to Papa's room, I note the half-eaten plate of cookies on his bedside table. As I approach, he struggles to lift his eyelids. "Marshmallow? I thought you ran a bakery now."

His confusion cracks through the protective layer carefully built around my heart. "Papa, I told you to stop eating these cookies. Mama has made important changes to your diet. You need to follow them if you want to get better."

"Nonsense. The children love a chubby St. Nick. I always eat cookies this time of year."

Handing the plate to my mother, I lock eyes with her. "Mama, I'm telling you, in no uncertain terms, do not let father eat any more of these Linzer cookies."

She takes the plate and stares at the cookies before gazing up at me. "What's going on?"

"I'll bake Papa a batch of gingerbread cookies before I leave. Other than those specific cookies or any healing potions you create, allow no one to enter this room or deliver any food."

She squares her shoulders. "I am the queen of the Pole, young lady."

My bravery wavers in the face of my powerful queen mother.

"You are. Artikoa and I spent two years among humans. I'm sure I don't have to remind you the persecution you suffered before you met father and the two of you created this magical place. Something isn't right. I don't have time to figure out what that is, but Artikoa will investigate while I deliver toys. We wanted to spare you this information, but you have a right to know. There could be foul play."

Her gentle eyes flash with immense power. "How? Who in my kingdom would dare turn against the saint?"

Kissing her cheek softly, I grasp both of her shoulders as I reply. "I'll find out. Promise me you'll protect Papa until Arti and I finish our investigation. Trust me, Mama. I'm good at this."

She clutches my arms and chokes back a sob. "Cynthia, you're twice the elf I could ever be. I know you will succeed in spreading joy throughout the world." She sniffs sharply. "Not just tonight. Your heart is too full for simply one night. Don't worry, I'll take care of your papa."

The three of us slip from the room as Papa falls into fitful slumber.

Mama wanders into her library to research the healing lore of her people, while I whip up the quickest batch of gingerbread cookies in history.

It hardly helps things that Artikoa paces during my entire baking ritual.

"Don't you have somewhere to be, Arti?"

"My top priority is protecting Santa. And today

that means you. Once you're safely in that sleigh, I'll start my investigation. Until then, I am your white shadow."

Despite the tension, his white shadow comment causes me to giggle uncontrollably. Even Arti allows himself a brief chuckle.

When the last tray of cookies comes out of the oven, I package everything up and tie a special red bow.

"No one touches this except Mama. Promise me."

He tucks his left paw under and bows low. "I swear on my life, Your Highness."

CHAPTER 13

*M*ama helps me into my suit before standing back to admire Thimble's work. She takes a minute to wipe tears from her eyes. "You look so much like your father, Cynthia. If I didn't know better . . ."

"Thank you, Mama. You take care of Papa, and I'll make sure every one of the presents gets delivered. We'll save Christmas — together."

She hugs me tight and leaves my room without another word.

Artikoa insists on walking me to the sleigh. "We can't risk any further delays. Do you have everything you need?"

Patting the left pocket of my suit, I nod. "I

have the sleep dust here, in case any children surprise me." I pat the right pocket and chuckle. "And I have two spare gingerbread cookies in case I get peckish — in flight."

I don't believe I've ever seen the arctic fox roll his eyes before, but he absolutely does. "With cookies and milk at every stop along the way, how could you possibly get peckish?"

"You have me terrified, Artikoa. I probably won't eat any of those things. Of course, I'll make sure it looks like Santa ate them, but think about what you said. Alcohol? Sedatives? What did you expect?"

"I did not intend to cause a fear response, Cynthia. My goal was to keep you safe and informed."

"Well, you've managed to do all three. We have to get going. If I don't get that sleigh in the air in the next ten minutes, we'll already be behind schedule."

Arti bounds from my room and leads the way to the loading area at the rear of the factory.

My heart soars when I see the glossy red sleigh pulled by nine amazing reindeer. The loading crew puts the finishing touches on the bag, as well as running the final test on the navigation equipment as I approach.

"Are we ready, good elves?"

The flight captain makes a quick bow, glances at me, and falls speechless.

"Is there a problem, Captain?"

"Santa? Is that you?"

Attempting to mimic my father's jolly laugh, I dip my head in the captain's direction. "It's me. Cynthia. In a beautifully made suit by Thimble."

He swallows hard, and there's still a hint of doubt in his eyes, but it's clear he believes me. Elves can't lie. "Everything is ready, Santa."

The captain leads a brief cheer, and I walk toward the lead reindeer, Chip. Holding the joyous memories of flying in the sleigh with Papa, I stroke my hand across Chip's back. He immediately lifts into the air with such power that he pulls the reindeer behind him off their forelegs.

Holding this precious magic, I continue down the team, stroking each of the reindeer in turn. Finally, I struggle to climb into a sleigh that is already taking flight.

Artikoa yips once from the ground, and I lean over the side. "Any parting advice, Most Venerable Elder?"

He lifts his pointed nose toward the reins in my hand. "The magic is potent this evening, Cynthia. I believe you can send it through the reins, directly to each harness. It will speed things up."

The sleigh is pulling away from the ground like a hot-air balloon receiving puffs of fiery heat. Waving to the ground crew and *my* most trusted advisor, I call into the night air as the dome opens above me. "Merry Christmas! And to all, a good night!"

A fading cheer of Merry Christmas vanishes as the dome closes behind us. The crisp polar air adds speed to our journey.

"To Spitsbergen!" The veteran reindeer seem to know the route even better than me. From there, they easily continue on our special journey with little help from me.

As we glide above the Caspian Sea, my stomach churns, and sweat soaks into the fake beard. My inner rebel would love to toss the disguise into the glistening waters below, but my duty to Santa comes first.

A blast of frosty air cools my skin and renews my resolve. "For Santa," I shout to the team. The jangle of bells on their harnesses is the only response from the reindeer.

Things are going well, and I'm over halfway through the gift-delivery route. My rosy cheeks lift as I marvel at the beauty of the Acropolis. Landing on a domed roof of a krypsona on Santorini, I find a mound of baklava beside their small tree. It appears to be an olive tree in a hand-painted pot, but there are tiny lights and small handmade ornaments.

The baklava smells divine, although my stomach is still causing trouble. But the glistening orange-scented honey syrup is irresistible.

I only meant to eat one, but the crispy phyllo pastry and the gooey walnut filling are too much to resist. As I pop the final piece into my mouth, a bleary-eyed Greek girl stumbles from a nearby bedchamber.

Her warm-brown eyes fill with shock and awe.

In a flash, I grab a pinch of sleep dust from my pocket and blow it at the small lass. "Merry Christmas, Eleni."

Quick as a wink, I'm back in the sleigh, sending dreams of flight through the harnesses. The reindeer take flight and we finish our route with no further mistakes.

As we approach the North Pole's protective magical dome, I can discern no opening. Strange! Mama always senses Papa's return. Perhaps my energy isn't enough.

The team and I circle the bubble twice. No opening appears.

I set the empty sleigh and the hard-working reindeer down in a field just outside the dome.

Approaching the magical sphere, I lightly tap. Here's hoping someone inside will realize we've returned.

I foolishly have no means of communicating with my mother.

Wait! I do have something! I still have the key in the pocket of my sweatpants.

Tugging at the thick black belt, I lift the edge of the velvet coat, reach under the velvet pants, and search the pocket of my sweats.

"Jingle bells!" I have the key to Mama's garden. It may not be a snow globe, but my mother created it with her magic. If I can send a pulse of energy, or anything really, through this key, it may alert my mother.

Turning to the team, I reassure them and apologize for the delay.

They seem undisturbed. A few of them paw at the snow, searching for lichen or other tasty treats.

Clasping the key softly between my hands, I close my eyes and think of Mama. "Mama, I know you're watching over Papa, but I need your help. I need you to open a door. The team and I are on the ground outside the reindeer paddock. Please, Mama, I need you."

A moment later, the dome wall in front of me shimmers. A large arch-shaped portion vanishes.

"Thank you, Mama."

Hurrying back to the sleigh, I aim the reindeer for the opening and they calmly plod through. Without the excitement of toy delivery, I can hear the gentle click clack as they walk forward. Folks may think it's simply poetic to refer to the click-ety-clack of Santa's sleigh. The truth is, reindeer have a special tendon above their hooves that click clacks over the bone in what we would call their ankle. The sound helps keep the herd together in thick fog or heavy snow. This fact is one of the many things people assume are fantasy or myth about Santa. If you knew the whole story, like I do, you'd be surprised how close the songs come to the reality.

As the back of the sleigh slips through the dome, I actually feel the magic close behind me.

Glad to be home, I'm surprised there's no sign of my mother or any of the landing crew elves.

As I reach out to open the large gate in the paddock, Zig and Zag come racing across the snow.

"Santa! We were waiting at the landing zone. A thousand pardons."

I wave away their apologies with one gloved hand. "Not to worry, Zig and Zag. We were forced to use an alternate entrance. The team performed to perfection. Your training proved impeccable.

And Chip here is a rising star in his own right. Excellent selection of reindeer."

One bows while the other curtsies. Zig and Zag each grab one side of Chip's harness and lead the team into the stable.

"I'll leave this in your capable hands. Have either of you seen Artikoa?" The pair turns in unison. "Not since your departure, Santa."

Pulling off the flowing wig and lush beard, I wave to the elves as I trudge toward home.

Tonight, the streets are fairly quiet. A random elf wanders here or there, but most of the hardworking folks are home in bed, grabbing a few hours of slumber before the huge community breakfast under our centuries-old North Pole Christmas tree.

As I turn the corner onto the cobblestone street leading to my home, Artikoa bounds toward me.

"Cynthia, did you eat those cookies in your pocket?"

Patting my pocket, I chuckle. "No. Thanks for reminding me." Reaching in, I pull out two slightly crumbled cookies and inhale deeply.

Arti leaps through the air and knocks the cookies from my hand.

"What in the North Pole, Arti?"

His hackles rise as he bares his teeth. "Your

instincts were correct. Your father's cookies are most certainly tainted. Yours may be as well."

Racing toward my house, I follow Artikoa to Papa's room, taking the stairs two at a time.

Mama sits at the side of his bed. A half-eaten plate of Linzer cookies rests on his night table.

"Mama! I told you not to give him any more cookies."

She can scarcely speak through her tears. "Not me. Someone— When I was opening the dome— I came back and—"

From her broken report, all I get is that someone snuck into our home while my mother helped the reindeer and I exit the dome for our gift-delivery mission.

"Mama, I know you don't want to believe anyone would purposely hurt Papa, but there's something wrong with these cookies. Something we can't explain. I have to investigate."

She sniffs and stares at the floor.

"Can you set a ward on his door? No one outside of the three of us can enter Papa's room until we find the culprit."

Stricken with fear, she raises her face and shakes her head. "Cynthia, do you know what you're saying? Elves are kind and honest. No elf would intentionally hurt your father."

I have no response at the moment. Turning to

Artikoa, I'm counting on a nugget of wisdom from the Most Venerable Elder. "What did you learn in your investigation?"

His amber eyes flare with protection. "I followed your hunch about the cookies and went straight to the bakery. Jelly mentioned that Willow is the younger sister of that upstart, Ash. That could be a dangerous connection. However, Jelly had no idea of Violet's family or where her kin may live. This bears further investigation, as well."

"What about the missing reindeer?"

The fox sniffs sharply. "I questioned additional reindeer, and they all said the same thing. The tenth reindeer didn't smell right and had vanished by morning."

"A bad smell isn't going to get us far. Was there anything else?"

Artikoa sighs. "Rudolph is blind and a bit hard of hearing, but his nose — that beautiful nose — still works. He claimed he hasn't smelled that scent in centuries, but he couldn't quite place it."

"What happened to this stinky reindeer, Arti? Someone would notice a reindeer wandering around the North Pole."

The wise fox sits back on his haunches and inhales sharply through his nose. "I feel we are dealing with a shape shifter. This elf, Willow, may be more than she seems."

Mama swipes at her tears, and sharp clarity returns to her emerald eyes. "I gave that elf a key to my greenhouse. Why would I do that?"

Now isn't the time to point fingers, so I hold my judgment. "Maybe she had some power. What did she want in the greenhouse?"

Mama shrugs her fine, elven shoulders. "No idea. She always went without me. I can't believe I let a stranger enter my greenhouse — alone!"

Flashing through the memories of my tour with Mama, a strange picture comes into focus. "The castor beans! You said the soil had been disturbed. What else can they be used for besides the turkey-red oil?"

The color drains from Mama's features, and she collapses onto the bed.

Her shaky hand presses against her amulet as she chokes back emotion. "Ricin. Almost every part of the castor bean plant is poisonous."

It only takes a second for me to apply what I've learned in the human world to our current dilemma. "Mama, someone or *something* is trying to kill Papa. I'll bet you anything they laced these Linzer cookies with ricin." My chest squeezes tight. "Artikoa and I will find Willow. You put up that ward to protect Papa."

She nods emphatically.

"Now that you know about the ricin, can you —" Hope aches in my chest. "Can you heal Papa?"

She reaches for my hand and squeezes it with all the strength she possesses. "I am the fairy queen, my darling. Eons of healing knowledge have passed from one queen to the next. I will find a way to save the saint." She squares her shoulders. "And then we'll bring this foul creature to justice."

CHAPTER 14

*D*etermination and a sliver of hope surge through the three of us as we slip from Papa's room. Mama clutches her amulet, delicately swirls her hand, and magic crackles across the doorway.

"No one outside the three of us will enter that room — and live."

Sharp prickles, like cold snow falling down the back of my coat, poke my skin. I've never heard my mother speak so harshly. "We'll find her, Mama."

Artikoa bounds toward the front door. When I glance over my shoulder, my powerful mother is moving with shocking precision as she gathers ingredients and scans the page of one of her many tomes of fairy lore.

Outside the door, Artikoa gazes upward, and in unison we exclaim, "The bakery!"

As we hurry toward my favorite place at the North Pole, an inappropriate chuckle escapes.

The wise elder utters a little growl, which echoes off the cobblestone. "You find this humorous?"

"No, not at all. It was— For a minute, we sounded like Zig and Zag."

The pure white fox tilts his head, acknowledges the accuracy of my comment, and continues toward our destination.

We burst into the bakery, as Jelly closes for the night. "Goodness! I was about to step into the back room to catch a few winks before the celebration. Do you two need more cookies?"

Arti darts past her to search the back room.

Words spill from my worried mouth. "For your safety, and the safety of all of Santa's elves, I'm going to have to ask you to throw out all of your inventory. Including any pre-made dough or icing you may have in the back."

Her gentle brown eyes widen. "What in the North Pole?"

An elf screams.

Willow emerges with a stone container in her hands, and a vengeful arctic fox at her back.

Jelly gasps. "Most Venerable Elder! Don't hurt her!"

Artikoa leaps onto the counter and pushes in, barely two inches from Jelly's face. "If Cinnamon were here, she would understand. We have a killer loose in the North Pole. Willow found this container hidden under Violet's cot."

Jelly shakes her head. "What? Why?"

Artikoa continues. "The box contains a residue of white powder known as ricin. Willow claims she's innocent of any wrongdoing."

My head is exploding with questions. "Willow, do you swear on the amulet of Queen Erregina that you weren't poisoning Santa?"

Willow breaks into heart-wrenching sobs. "Never. I swear on my mother's sapling."

This is the strongest oath a forest elf can swear. "Then why? Why were you helping Violet make ricin?"

Willow swipes at her tears and shakes her head furiously. "I wasn't. I would never! That elf has some power over my brother, but I never trusted her. She must've stolen the key from me. She always sent me to get the reindeer milk and handled the pick up from the greenhouses on her own."

Jelly sputters, coughs, clears her throat, and says nothing. She seems too shocked to speak.

Artikoa jumps in. "What do you know about the castor bean, Willow?"

"Nothing. Why?"

"My ma— Queen Erregina said you were working on a new shampoo for the reindeer that used turkey-red oil."

Willow's tiny button nose scrunches up. "Me? I'm allergic to reindeer. Violet was always the one working late on her private projects."

"Why did the queen give you a key to her private greenhouse?" My heart thuds in my chest. What if Willow is working with Violet?

"I have no idea, Your Highness. I never asked for it. One day your mother came to the door to accept a delivery and she handed me the key. I took it without question. She's the queen." Willow bobbed a small curtsy.

Glancing at Artikoa, I press a hand to my chest. "Willow is telling the truth, Arti. If Violet lied to my mother — and who knows how many other elves — it explains how she worked under-cover for so many weeks."

Artikoa growls. "Violet was certainly mixing the poisonous powder from that container into the raspberry jam, and perhaps the icing for the gingerbread cookies." He gives me a meaningful grumble. "We know she's been regularly delivering these poison Linzer cookies to Santa. She even slipped something into the icing, or the gingerbread cookies, she made for Cindy. Throw out everything. My apologies to you and the entire Roll family. But too many lives are at stake."

Jelly bows her head reverently. "As you command, Most Venerable Elder. Please forgive my impertinence."

Reaching across the counter, I pat her shoulder. "It's okay. It's pretty unbelievable. We have to find Violet. Where does she live?"

Jelly swallows with difficulty as she glances from me to Artikoa and back. "I thin— I don't actually know."

"Who are her kin?"

The young elf pats her chest and struggles to draw breath. "I have no idea! She came in, told us she was a great baker, and mother hired her on the spot."

Tears spring to her eyes, and she clutches my hand. "You know what it's like, Cindy. It's the North Pole! We don't check references. We're Santa's elves. Not because we have to be, but because our good queen loves him and so do we. If I—" Harsh sobs wrack her compact frame.

"Don't fret. We'll find her. Where does she go when she's not here?"

Jelly throws her small arms in the air. "She's always here. Violet has a cot in the back. I thought it was because she loved to bake." Jelly's voice cracks as she collapses onto a stool behind the counter and drops her head into her pudgy, flour-covered hands.

"Arti, the greenhouse! We know Violet goes to the greenhouse."

He leaps from the counter in a single graceful arc. I follow him out the door, calling apologies and encouragement to Jelly as we go.

"Arti, if my cookies, or my icing, were poisoned, why didn't I get sick?" As soon as my words hit the air, I remember the grumbling tummy aches and the sweaty face. "Wait, I did get sick. But why am I better?"

Artikoa pauses, and his wise amber eyes seem to stop time. "Perhaps your odd combination of blood gave the poison a run for its money. As soon as you stopped eating the tainted treats, it appears you began to heal." He tilts his head a quarter-turn. "We'll know more when your mother cures Santa." With that he bounds toward the farm.

Mama's greenhouse is secure when we arrive. Arti snarls and grinds his teeth together. "Wait here."

Without concern for my response, he bounds into the toolshed and returns a moment later with a gleaming piece of metal between his teeth.

Taking the lock, I scrunch up my face. I have no idea what he's doing.

"You have a key, don't you, Cynthia?"

Searching through my pocket, I grab the key and hold it up.

"Remove that lock and replace it with this one. Keep both keys."

"Good idea." As I make the switch, I add, "I'm glad to know that no further poisons will be extracted and used against my people."

Artikoa takes the compromised lock and tosses it into a bed of lemon balm.

"We must sound the alarm. The clock is ticking, and we need all the help we can get."

"Agreed."

Racing to the massive Christmas tree in the center of our protected village, Artikoa commandeers the loudspeakers used to broadcast Christmas carols.

"Good elves. This is Artikoa, Most Venerable Elder. I regret to inform you we have a criminal in our midst. This culprit is posing as an elf named Violet. Last seen working at the bakery. The elf must be found. I need every able-bodied elf to take to the streets and locate this vile creature."

Without a moment's delay, doors open and elves flood onto the cobblestone.

It's pure chaos.

Arti sighs and returns to the intercom. "Elves with the names from A to E search the eastern quadrant. Elves with names from F to L search the southern quadrant. Elves with names from M to S search the western quadrant. Elves with names from T to Z search the northern quadrant."

It takes a few minutes for the elves to rearrange themselves, but they love rules and solutions, so they eagerly take Artikoa's advice and begin searching.

The two of us stand helplessly in the center of the village.

Shrugging, I ask, "Do we search, or should we stay here?"

Artikoa shakes his shoulders and rises onto his hind legs to sniff the air. "Follow me!"

He starts off in a northeasterly direction, and it's all I can do to keep up.

We dash between elves, down narrow streets, and finally through someone's backyard. When we reach the base of the dome, I see what Artikoa smelled.

Violet is hacking away at the magic dome with a pickax she must've stolen from the factory.

Ash, the leader of the forest clan, is on his

knees in the snow. "Please, Violet, don't leave. I promise I'll free my clan and follow you back to the old country." His voice cracks. "I need more time, my darling."

Violet acts as though Ash has ceased to exist. She continues to hack at the magical dome as she snarls, "You serve no purpose now, fool. You and your impotent clan were merely a distraction for the queen."

Ash's glazed eyes seem to see only love. "Let me make it up to you, love."

Violet turns from her hacking on the dome and scowls with disdain. "I have failed. Santa lives. Can you change that, pathetic elf?"

Artikoa growls and lunges forward. A small arctic hare hops out of his way.

Violet turns to face him, wielding the axe as a weapon.

A resonant buzzing fills the air that reminds me of the last time Artikoa transformed.

Holding my breath, I'm about to duck for cover when the tiny bunny before him morphs into an eight-foot-tall polar bear. The bear lumbers toward the pickax-wielding Violet as she transforms before our eyes. Twisting horns sprout from her head, and her face melts into a creature of nightmares. Her once tiny shoulders grow broad and are covered with dirty, matted fur . . . A Krampus!

"Of course! That's what Rudolph meant, Arti. He led the last team to work with the Krampus before Papa ended the partnership."

The brave fox circles back to protect me. "No harm will come to you, Your Highness."

"What about Ash?" My heart goes out to the elven leader. The Krampus most certainly magically manipulated him.

The raging white bear slaps the Krampus with a dangerous paw, and the pickax flies harmlessly into the snow. Thankfully, missing Ash.

The Krampus lowers her twisted horns and growls. "My kin will find a way to dispose of Santa and force the heir to acknowledge us!" it shouts as it prepares to charge. "I am one of many!"

The bear opens his massive jaw and leaps to meet her.

Before the titans connect, a flash of bright-blue magic suspends them both in mid air.

Hundreds of elves have gathered, and I worry I should rush them off to safety. Instead, the sea of pointed ears parts to make way for the powerful form of the queen. As Queen Erregina marches between them, all heads bow.

Her amulet glows brighter than the evening star.

She addresses the gigantic bear. "Pom-pom,

you've performed your duties admirably. Please return to your guardianship form."

Swirls of golden stardust surround the polar bear, and, where a ferocious beast once reared, a tiny arctic hare hops away into the snow.

Now is my chance to grab Ash and drag him from harm's way.

The queen approaches the still-suspended Krampus. "Violet, or whatever is your true name, you've failed. My elves are no longer warring creatures, but we will not tolerate attacks on our sacred dome. Nor will we stand by while evil attempts to trounce good."

She turns to the elves gathered, and, in a thundering voice I don't recognize, she announces, "Santa lives. Even now he is recovering from the hideous poison this foul creature used against him. Christmas is saved, good elves."

A thunderous cheer erupts as tears burst from my eyes.

While I struggle to let down my guard, a commotion behind my mother strangles the breath in my throat.

The Krampus has slipped from the magical trap. It lunges forward as Artikoa transforms into his protective yeti form beside me. My heart knows he intends to sacrifice himself to save the queen, but Mama has other plans.

She spins on her tiny heels, and a flash of midnight-blue magic explodes from her amulet. The hideous Krampus, with her twisted horns, one human foot, and one cloven hoof, vanishes like a dying star.

All present shield their eyes from the overwhelming display of power.

The flash of energy dissipates. Hundreds, if not thousands, of bright elves stare at my mother in awe.

Ash, finally in possession of his senses, shouts, "All hail, Queen Erregina!" He falls to his knees and bows so low his face touches the snow.

Like a wave crashing on the shore, the gathered masses fall to their knees from the front row to the back.

Mama turns and motions for me to join her.

"Rise, good elves. You are safe. We have my daughter to thank for solving this mystery."

"All hail, Princess Cynthia!" The crowd cheers until my mother finally gestures for quiet.

She lifts her chin and addresses her subjects. "It's no secret that I did not support her desire to enter the human world. I now announce to all gathered here, I was wrong." A murmur of distress swirls through the crowd. "Yes, it is possible for even the queen to be misinformed. If my brilliant daughter had not experienced the good and bad humans have to offer, we may not have solved this horrible puzzle in time to save our beloved St. Nicholas."

Tears are already streaming down my face, but, when my mother steps to the side and bends a curtsy to me, I weep. I've never felt this acceptance from her.

I'm fortunate that weeping openly in front of the city of elves will not be judged by these kind, gentle creatures.

Struggling to swallow and find my voice, I reach out a hand and pull mother to her feet. "Please note, good elves, that it was the healing magic of your queen that brought Santa back from the brink."

Further cheers ripple through the crowd, and Mama slips an arm around my waist. "I believe it is time to begin the celebration. Please, join me in a cheer of Merry Christmas."

A multitude of voices join in unison as the cheer, "Merry Christmas, good elves!" echoes inside the dome.

The healing magic for Papa and the battle with the Krampus have taken a toll on Mama. She leans heavily on me as we thread our way through the crowd, joining in on Christmas carols here and there.

"I must return to the house, Cynthia. I need rest."

Artikoa remains to oversee the festivities, and I walk Mama back to our home. As I reach to open the front door, it pulls from my grasp.

The ruddy-cheeked figure of Papa fills the doorway. "Marshmallow!"

CHAPTER 15

Throwing my arms around Papa's neck, all the emotions I've been holding in spill forth. "I thought we were going to lose you, Papa."

"Nonsense, Marshmallow. My angel blood was working overtime to replace each cell that the poison killed. Once your mother cleared the poison from my system, I could finally get the upper hand. Then celestial healing took over. You and your mother are a formidable team."

Mama yawns loudly and kisses the top of Papa's head. "I need to lie down for a minute. But don't you two let me sleep all day. I have a present for Cynthia."

At the word present, my not-pointed ears perk

right up. "Are you sure you can't stay a few more minutes?"

My mother shakes her head and yawns a second time. "Not a chance. I'll see you both in a few hours."

Once she disappears upstairs, Papa insists on hearing every detail of the Christmas gift delivery adventure. His smile is bright as he leans his ear my way.

When I get to the part about the baklava on Santorini, he grips his round belly with both hands and lets out a loud, "Ho ho ho." The pink in his cheeks brightens as he continues. "That Eleni Katsaros has been trying to catch me for three years running. She is a determined little thing. Please tell me you didn't use too much sleep dust on her." A hint of worry tightens his jolly grin.

"Only the tiniest pinch, Papa. She'll be awake for Christmas morning with no problem."

We share a chuckle. "Did you find all the stockings hung in a row?"

"I did, Papa. It took some getting used to — creeping down chimneys with that pack of toys."

He grins. "You slipped everything under each tree?"

"Of course! And I whispered what I was bringing as I placed each gift. You still do that, right?"

Santa cups my face in his hands. "You dear young girl! You did everything perfectly. I couldn't be more proud. You saved Christmas, Cindy. The world was fast asleep, and you made the magic happen. The legend of jolly old Saint Nic lives on."

This tender moment between us warms my heart, but the mood quickly shifts as I reach the part in the story when we revealed Violet to be another Krampus.

"They are growing bold. Entering my domain to make such a deadly attack—" My father's voice stops abruptly as he strokes his thick, white beard.

"Papa, what will you do? There's only one of you, and we have no idea how large the Krampus clan has become."

"Your mother and I will add security measures anytime the dome is opened. I'm not worried about things here at the North Pole." He places a caring hand on my knee. "I'm worried about you, Marshmallow. I assume you're heading back to the human world."

Even though I knew this moment would come, I've been dreading the discussion. "Yes, Papa. I'll be returning to Silver Shoals. But not today. I want to enjoy Christmas with my family."

Getting to my feet, I lean over and kiss Papa's head as my mother had. "Now you get upstairs and get some rest, Santa. You may be half-angel, but you're still half-human. We'll all get together for a late Christmas breakfast after you and Mama are feeling up to it."

He gets to his feet with an uncharacteristic groan. "Perhaps you're right, Marshmallow. I'm not quite myself." Papa walks toward the stairs and twists to look back at me. "I was hoping you'd make some of those miniature cheesecakes you invented, eh?"

"I'll make anything you want, Papa. Go get some rest."

As I stand alone in the kitchen, a wave of exhaustion washes over me, but it's not enough to send me upstairs. My body may be tired, but my thoughts are spinning. A pleasant walk under the aurora borealis should put things right.

Changing into my own clothes, I slip on a pair of striped leggings and an old sweatshirt with Frosty the Snowman on the front. Another legendary figure at the North Pole. After one too many close calls with early spring thaws, Frosty took up permanent residence under our dome.

Outside, the streets are deserted. Every elf in our wonderful village is at the Christmas tree enjoying fluffy pancakes, tern-egg quiches, and whatever sweet treats Jelly could put together in the limited time she had once Arti and I forced her to dump all her inventory.

I still feel a bit terrible about that, but I would've felt worse if anyone else had been — injured.

The echo of Christmas carols sung by thousand of joyous elf voices fills the dome. Wandering through glowing streets, I gaze up at the northern lights and smile. There really is no better place on earth to view this magical display.

At last, I arrive at the scene of the showdown between Violet, Pom-pom, and my mother.

There's no sign of the feisty arctic hare, but there are certainly tracks and gouges in the snow.

A shimmering glow reflects off the snow, and a flicker catches my eye. Stepping forward, I reach down and recover the handmade broom pin with a single golden twig.

Odd. I definitely remember seeing this on Violet's top. When Mama blinked her from existence, I thought everything would've vanished. Her clothing and her elf boots are nowhere to be seen. Why would this little pin survive?

Turning it back and forth in my hand, I don't see anything remarkable about it. I'll ask my mother tomorrow.

Slipping the pin in my pocket, I meander toward home. The walk has done its trick, and I'm more than ready for bed.

As I trudge up the cobblestone, a familiar flash

of white fur catches my eye. "Artikoa! I thought you were at the celebration?"

He pauses outside our front door. "I came to check on you. I wasn't sure how quickly you'd be returning to Silver Shoals."

"Don't worry, Arti, I won't leave without you."

My comment clearly flusters the arctic elder. He shifts his weight from one paw to the other and shakes thoroughly, as though he's drying off after a quick bath. "That was not my concern, Cynthia. I simply wanted an update from Santa and a clear timeline. Nothing more."

"Whatever you say, Arti. I'm headed upstairs for a short nap. Then I have to make a batch of miniature cheesecakes for Papa before we exchange gifts."

"Do you have a gift for your family?"

"I haven't had time to think about it. I've been so preoccupied with all my Christmas Eve duties." Tapping a finger on my lip, a solution pops to mind.

"I suppose the cheesecakes can be my gift to Papa. And—" As I shove my hands in the pocket of my sweatshirt, my fingers bump the small metal pin. "Oh, and I have an idea what I might give Mama."

"Very well. I'm sure your father will notify me when you're ready to depart."

"If I didn't know better, I'd say you're eager to get back to Silver Shoals."

He attempts to shrug off my comment. "I'm simply concerned about leaving Cinnamon Roll in the human world. After all, she is an elf. Should anyone ask her outright, she'd be unable to lie."

Melting snowballs!

CHAPTER 16

*P*ushing thoughts of Silver Shoals from my head, I lose myself in baking. My happy place. My escape from reality.

Sure, I could've used a couple more winks of sleep, but it's Christmas Day! I don't want to miss any of it.

While Mama and Papa recharge, I whip up the best batch of miniature cheesecakes I've ever made! There's something about *dulce de leche* made with reindeer milk that just can't be duplicated in the human world. The pecans from the greenhouse are so fragrant, and toasting them adds a lovely caramelization that pairs beautifully with the *dulce de leche*.

I pop the treats in the oven, set a timer, and

stir myself a fresh pot of peppermint hot chocolate.

Papa is the first to emerge.

"Marshmallow, is that what I think it is?"

"Oh, Papa! You've spoiled your Christmas surprise." I wink and chuckle as he walks across the kitchen to give me a hug.

"You know better than trying to surprise Santa. I'm confident you're not planning on making me wait until they've chilled for two hours." His mischievous eyes twinkle.

"Since you already know what I'm planning to give you as a present, I may as well serve it to you warm. Even though I can assure you, they taste better after they've been chilled."

He waves away my comment. "There will be plenty. I'll get to have them both ways. Best of both worlds, right?"

There's a deeper meaning in his gaze. He's referring to me living with one foot in the human world and one foot at the North Pole. "I've enjoyed my visit, Papa. I have to admit, I'm excited to return to Silver Shoals. The bakery is doing so well, and I've made wonderful friends."

He gestures toward the simmering pot of peppermint hot chocolate, and I quickly scoop some into a mug.

"Join me at the table, Marshmallow."

Uh oh. Some of the most uncomfortable discussions of my youth happened at this kitchen table, over mugs of peppermint hot chocolate.

When I take a seat next to my father, he puts a hand on top of mine and gives a little squeeze. "Your mother tells me there's a special young man. How special?"

I feel fifty-three all over again. My cheeks instantly turn a rosy red, and I cast my gaze downward. "Oh, Papa, don't start. Keith and I barely know each other."

"According to your mother, you spend a great deal of time with this Keith Winters. Now, he's obviously on the Nice List, but what do you really know about his family?"

"His family? It hasn't come up. We've been on a few dates, and we live in the same building. I don't think we're at the point of him taking me to meet his family."

My father takes a long sip of hot cocoa and wipes the whipped cream from his mustache. "Good. Take things slow. When you live as long as we do, one has to be careful who you hitch your sleigh to."

"Don't worry, Papa. Keith is a kind human. He works hard to help his community. You'd like him."

Santa leans forward, and another twinkle in his

eye captures my attention. "When will I have the pleasure of meeting Mr. Winters?"

The blush instantly returns to my cheeks. "Papa!" The timer on the stove saves me from any further embarrassment.

"Give me a minute to decorate them."

Papa wiggles his shoulders with childlike excitement. "Okay, Marshmallow, but don't take too long."

Adding a healthy scoop of *dulce de leche* to each cheesecake, I sprinkle some toasted pecans, and finish with a drizzle of dark-chocolate ganache.

I stand back and admire my creation. Placing four of the still-warm miniature cheesecakes on a plate, I present them to my father with a slight curtsy. "Merry Christmas, Santa."

He leans forward, kisses me on the cheek, and eagerly accepts the plate.

Quick as a wink, the cheesecakes vanish. "You are truly gifted! I hope those humans appreciate what they've got."

"They do, Papa. They do."

Santa leans back in the chair and utters a sigh of contentment. "I suppose you'll be wanting your present." He chuckles, and his belly jiggles like a bowl full of jelly.

"You have a present for me? How? You were sick."

He strokes his shimmering white beard and winks. "Santa would never forget his only daughter."

Papa reaches into a small velvet satchel tied to his waist and extracts a truly remarkable feather. It's over a foot long and is the purest white I've ever seen. "Oh, Papa, it's breathtaking."

He sniffs sharply and wipes a tear from his eye. "This is a feather from my mother's wing. My father left it for me in a locked chest. After he passed away, I found the feather and a letter explaining how my mother was an angel, and had to return to heaven when I was born. She left this feather behind so I would never forget the true story of my birth."

He extends the feather toward me, and I accept it with hushed reverence. "Papa, are you sure you want me to have this? Is it safe to take this into the human world?"

My father unties the bag from his waist belt and lays it on the table. "Your mother made this pouch for me. It's similar to the present bag I use on Christmas Eve."

Glancing at the small pouch, I begin to understand. This large feather will vanish into the small bag. "Am I the only one who can remove it from the bag, Papa?"

"Only you, me, and my heavenly mother. Although, I doubt she will return to earth."

Turning the feather over, I marvel at its absolute purity. In fact, it doesn't even cast a shadow. "Papa! The feather casts no shadow."

"That is correct. It is pure light. No darkness."

As I continue to marvel at the gift, Papa tells me more.

"I'm sure it has more properties than I will ever know, but the one thing my father mentioned in the note is that it could stop time. I've never used it for such a purpose. Perhaps it will serve you in your dealings in the human world — provide a measure of protection. Something I can't do from the North Pole."

The moment Papa tells me the secret of the feather, it seems to take on extra weight. As though it were made from gold or — what's heavier than gold? "Thank you, Papa. I will treasure this and take extra good care of it. I promise."

As I slip the feather into the little pouch, my mother enters the kitchen. Her eyes are bright, her flaxen ponytail smooth and high. "How did you like the present, Cynthia?"

"It's marvelous. And I love this pouch you made, Mama."

She fetches a glass of water and joins us at the

table. "Well, that was part of your father's gift to you. I have a different present for my talented daughter."

Receiving compliments from my mother that aren't immediately followed by a criticism is a whole new thing. I'm left speechless, almost.

"You don't have to give me a present. Spending Christmas at the North Pole was gift enough."

"Nonsense. It's Christmas. I have a proper gift for you."

Waving my hands quickly, I interrupt. "Wait. I have something for you."

My mother, looking somewhat surprised, exchanges an unreadable glance with my father. "How thoughtful, Cynthia."

Fishing around in the pocket of my hoodie, I retrieve the handmade birch-handled broom pin with its single golden twig among the broomcorns. "I didn't have time to wrap it. I apologize for the presentation, Mama."

In keeping with the positive mood, she clearly swallows her criticism.

Reaching across the table, I drop the pin into my mother's outstretched palm. Her initial reaction is a flash of fear. "Cynthia! You should've warned me."

"Sorry." I shake off the flustered feeling and

continue, "I wish I could've recovered the key you gave her, but—"

Mama bites her bottom lip. "No need to fret, Cynthia. I called the magic of that key back to me as I dispatched the hideous Krampus. It was my mistake to correct."

A simple nod acknowledges her admission. Pointing to the birchwood pin, I try to lighten the mood. "I want you to keep this token, Mama. I want you and everyone at the North Pole to remember the day you saved us. The day you saved Christmas."

She lays the pin on the table and wipes tears from her eyes. "We all worked together, my darling. Your father's angel blood, Artikoa's sharp senses, your brilliant sleuthing skills, and a pinch of my magic."

My cheeks lift with joy. "And let's not forget Pom-pom! How many other shape-shifting protectors inhabit the Pole?"

"It's probably best if you don't know. The fact that they live in secret is what makes them so effective." Her wise green eyes hold depths of mystery I can never hope to solve.

"Well, I better head upstairs and take a nap before Artikoa and I return to Silver Shoals."

Mama swallows hard, and I can only imagine

how difficult it is for her to accept the news that I won't be staying in the village.

"Cynthia, there's—"

"Mama, I don't want to ruin Christmas with a debate. Tomorrow morning, I'm returning to my bakery."

Her gentle laughter fills the room. "I suppose I deserved that. I was going to say, there's one more thing. My present for you, Marshmallow."

"Sorry, Mama. I thought— Never mind. What's my present?"

Returning to the table, I lean forward in anticipation.

Mama presents me with a small scroll.

"What is it?"

Mama grins. "Open it, silly girl."

Carefully unfurling the scroll, my breath catches in my throat. "Oh, wow! It's the ritual! Will I actually be able to see and hear Connie's ghost?"

"That's the idea. Be sure to let me know if it works, won't you?"

"Of course! How exciting! I can't wait to get home and try this out."

Mama gasps and clutches Papa's hand.

A moment too late, I realize my mistake. "My home *away* from home, Mama. No place on earth will ever replace the North Pole. You and Papa are my home."

She swallows hard, reaches across the table, and squeezes my hand with surprising strength for her slight frame.

"And you are our home, Marshmallow."

CHAPTER 17

Morning comes too soon. Artikoa and I have to leave the Christmas haven that is the North Pole and travel back to Silver Shoals. Mama dabs at a few tears, but Papa seems excited for me.

He twists his mustache, and his eyes twinkle. "Don't be a stranger, Marshmallow. You know you can pop home for a visit anytime."

"Thanks, Papa. I'll remember that. Maybe I can visit after the baby is born?"

"We'd love that." He hugs me tight, and his peppermint scent fills my heart with happiness. As I pull away, Papa whispers softly, "There were no instructions on how to use the feather, sweet girl. Trust your instincts. They've gotten you this far."

With that, he kisses my cheek, and he and Mama join hands. She places her left hand around her amulet and, quick as a wink, my arctic fox advisor and I are once again standing in my humble apartment in Silver Shoals.

"Arti, are we in the right place?"

He snorts as he chuckles. "Looks like Cinnamon Roll has *everything* under control. This place is neat as a pin."

Glancing around my sparkling clean apartment, I can't quite wrap my head around it. "Elves really do like to be tidy, don't they?"

Artikoa sniffs the air. "Perhaps we should check in on the bakery. I believe I smell something burning."

Dashing down the stairs without locking the apartment earns me a couple of yips from my overly cautious fox.

I mumble under my breath as we round the landing and descend the second flight of stairs. "There's no time, Arti."

When I enter the bakery, Jasmine nearly drops the coffee drink she's placing on the counter. "Cindy? When did you get back?"

Oops. "Just now. Thought I smelled something burning!" I dart into the back room before Jazz can ask any follow-up questions. Shock stops me in my tracks.

The back room of the bakery is the exact opposite of my apartment.

Flour dust covers nearly every flat surface. There's spilled icing, and even a few eggshells littering the floor.

"CR, is everything okay?"

The portly elf spins on her curled elf boots, and relief washes over her as she rushes toward me. "Cindy! I haven't been this thrilled to see you since that time you brought me the first batch of your miniature cheesecakes!" She throws her arms around my waist, and I curve down to return her greeting.

"Something is burning, CR."

"Jingle bells!" She scurries toward the oven, and I chuckle under my breath. I hadn't realized I'd picked up so many phrases from her.

"Tell you what, CR, how about I clean up while you make a new batch of whatever that was?"

My mentor tips the overly toasted gingerbread cookies into the trash and breathes a heavy sigh. "You'd think a 507-year-old elf would be able to handle a simple bakery. I had no idea how different things would be. I keep asking Mitch, down at the Wiggling Pig, for reindeer milk, and he stopped laughing at that joke after the fourth time."

Slipping a red apron over my head, I tie it snug and grab a dishrag. "You did an amazing job. We tossed you onto an iceberg without a paddle, CR. We'll get everything sorted today and send you home after dinner. Sound good?"

She presses a small hand to her chest and attempts to catch her breath. "That sounds lovely, Cindy. I've enjoyed this experience, but, if I never leave the North Pole again, it will be too soon."

As I'm about to share in her laughter, a familiar voice makes me choke on my chuckle.

"Cindy? Did I hear someone mention the North Pole?"

"Keith!" My feet turn toward him, and my arms want to squeeze him tight, but my traitorous rosy cheeks already display my level of discomfort with an audience.

As though he can read my mind, Keith closes the distance between us and hugs me tight. "Hiya, Cindy. I've missed you. I didn't get to give you your present. Can I make you dinner tonight? I have a great recipe for roasted vegetable lasagna."

This amazing guy! Maybe things are more serious than I could admit to Mama and Papa. "That sounds wonderful, but CR has to head back to the—"

"Yip. Yip."

Clearing my throat, I try again. "She's heading back home tonight. Can we have breakfast tomorrow?"

His beautiful green eyes sparkle. "So, coddled eggs for Artikoa, and I seem to remember you being a big fan of chocolate chip pancakes. Right?"

I could probably keep my apartment warm all winter with the glow of these cheeks. "I love pancakes! I can't believe you remembered."

He reaches out and grabs my hand in his. "I remember everything about you, Cindy."

If steam could come out of my ears like a boiling kettle, it would. This kind man is too much.

"I need to help Cinnamon Roll clean up the bakery. Thanks for stopping in. I'll see you tomorrow morning, okay?"

Keith smiles, and I swear there's a light blush on his cheeks as he leans in and plants a soft kiss on mine. "Looking forward to it."

The second he walks out of the back room, Cinnamon Roll whistles the opening chorus of "White Christmas," and we both giggle like young elves.

"What did you tell Santa about you and Mr. Winters?"

Busying myself with dusting, wiping, and polishing, I keep my answer short and sweet. "As little as possible, CR. As little as possible."

Artikoa carefully checks for humans within

earshot and mutters in his quietest tone, "I will be hunting if you need me."

"Okay, Arti. Thanks for all your help up north."

He gives a quick bow of his head. "My pleasure, Your Highness."

CR whips up a fresh batch of gingerbread cookies, and I finish cleaning, taking out the trash, and putting away all the pans. "Thanks again for taking care of the bakery while I was away."

She finishes stirring the icing, sets the bowl on the prep counter, and sidles up next to me. "So, Santa? Is he okay?"

Glancing over my shoulder, I suddenly feel the back room isn't safe. "We'll talk in the apartment. He's okay. But there's a bigger story."

I forgot how much elves enjoy gossip. CR rubs her hands together as though she's rolling a snickerdoodle in her palms. "Oooh, sounds good. I love a tasty tale."

"Hey, boss?"

CR and I reply in unison, "Yes?" We exchange a foolish glance and break into another round of giggles.

Jasmine walks into the back room and points directly at me. "Cindy, I was going to head out. You guys need any help in here?"

"I think we can handle it. Thank you very

much for all the help you gave Cinnamon Roll while I was away."

"No problem, boss. Everything okay at home?"

The simplest answer will be the best. "It is now. I was lucky I got home when I did. You are both lifesavers."

Jasmine shrugs her athletic shoulders and grins. "Hey, I made a few cups of coffee. It's not brain surgery."

Forcing a chuckle is the only thing that prevents me from spilling the candy canes about what actually happened at the North Pole.

Jasmine gives a casual wave as she heads out of the bakery.

Hanging my rag on the edge of the laundry hamper, I turn to Cinnamon Roll as I remove my apron. "Let's head upstairs and have dinner before you leave. Sorry, I don't have a present for you. Once you hear the full story, I'm sure you'll understand."

CR tosses her apron into the hamper, and beams. "Food and a story. Seems like you brought me a present after all."

Loading a plate with gingerbread cookies, extra icing, and miniature cheesecakes, my baking mentor, Cinnamon Roll, and I head upstairs.

"So you already know that Santa was ill, but let me tell you what really happened."

CR and I power through our meal of cookies and cakes as I regale her with the tale of trouble at the North Pole.

Of course, when I get to the part about Violet, CR is racked with guilt.

"Oh, Cindy! I feel like a foolish old elf. I should've suspected something immediately. I didn't even ask about her family. You know, kin is the most important thing to elves. She lied! She lied to me and I didn't notice."

CR wipes some icing from the corner of her mouth and dabs tears on her round cheeks.

Reaching across the table, I pat her arm. "It's not your fault. Elves can't lie. You had no reason to suspect Violet was anything other than what she claimed. There's never been a Krampus in the North Pole. No one recognized the signs. Not even your queen."

That last bit seems to soothe CR's spirit.

We polish off the last two cookies, and I hug her tight. "I promise to visit the North Pole at least once a year. I can't thank you enough for taking care of things here. Without your help, I might not have been able to solve the mystery. Santa might—"

Fresh tears spring to my eyes, and CR squeezes my hand. "Don't play the 'What if' game. That'll get you nowhere fast. Our wise queen always says the best question is, 'What now?' We can't dwell on what did or didn't happen. All we can change is what we do next. So you get back to running the best little bakery in Silver Shoals, and I'll start doing background checks on my new employees. Deal?"

She puts her right hand out like a regular human, and I shake it vigorously. "Deal."

CR brushes her hands together and smiles. "Done and dusted. Time to go home. Can you call Queen Erregina?"

Mother is in high spirits when she answers the snow globe. Papa has an arm around her, and the sight of his rosy cheeks makes my spirits soar. "You truly are jolly old St. Nicholas, Papa."

"Thanks to my brilliant daughter." He winks.

CR vanishes, and Mama blows me a kiss as the snow globe falls dark.

Still no sign of Artikoa. He must truly be enjoying the freedom outside the dome.

I best turn in for the night. I'll be up early making a batch of Connie's delicious fudge as a present for the equally yummy Keith Winters.

As I drift off to sleep, the gentle scrape of Arti's doggy door causes me to stir.

He leaps onto the end of the bed, circles twice, and lies down at my feet.

Best thing I can do is pretend to be asleep. It's no good letting him know I acknowledge his affections.

CHAPTER 18

I'm up before the sun, melting and mixing, so the fudge has time to set before I cut it into bite-size squares and wrap each square in a bit of Christmas-themed wax paper.

Artikoa yawns and treats himself to a big drink of water from his dish before he starts a conversation. "You're up early, Cynthia. Seems you may have brought a hint of the North Pole back to Silver Shoals."

"I'm having breakfast with Keith. I got up early to make some fudge to take as a gift. He mentioned something about having a present for me. I didn't have anything for him, so . . ."

The wise fox lets loose with a quiet howl. "An

official exchange of Christmas presents. This relationship is certainly escalating, Cynthia."

"Knock it off, Arti. I'm taking things nice and slow with Keith. Friends can exchange gifts."

There's a brief arch of one eyebrow before Arti slips out his access door with a soft snicker.

I treat myself to two mugs of peppermint cocoa and sample the fudge, before I wrap each individual piece and place them in a small basket with a pretty red bow.

I'm seated on the edge of my chair, wondering whether I should disturb Keith, when there's a soft knock at my door.

"Come in."

Keith opens the door, hangs his head, and exhales. "Geez, Cindy, you've got to lock your door. I'm not sure how they do it where you come from, but safety first. Okay?"

"You got it."

He takes one look at my red sweater with hand embroidered white snowflakes and my matching red leggings and nods. "You look wonderful. Come on over. The first batch of pancakes will be ready any minute." He scans my small apartment. "Where's your pup?"

I can't mention that Arti's probably hunting. "Artikoa won't be joining us."

For some reason that announcement makes Keith's eyes twinkle.

Scooping the basket off the table as I leave, I make a point of grabbing my keys off the hook and locking my door behind me.

Keith grins. "That's more like it. Come on in."

Once inside, he pulls my chair out for me, and I offer him the basket as I sit down.

"I made some fudge for you. Even though lemon drop cookies are your favorite, I'm sure you'll like this. It's Connie's most popular recipe at the bakery."

He accepts the basket. "Okey dokey. Let me get your gift."

Keith returns with a small package.

Gazing at the box, I think of Mama. My mother loves jewelry, and she was always fond of saying "The best things come in small packages." Surreptitiously crossing my fingers, I'm counting on luck to ward off the possibility of Keith getting me jewelry. I wear earrings once in a while, but, in general, jewelry isn't my thing.

"Go ahead and open it, Cindy. I'll grab the pancakes."

He disappears into his kitchen, but I've always been told not to open a gift without the giver present, so I wait for his return.

When he pops around the corner, he's balancing two loaded plates in one hand, and a large carafe of syrup in the other.

"There's butter on the table, and I heated the syrup. Do you also want some whipped cream?"

Inhaling deeply as he sets the delicious chocolate chip pancakes on the table in front of me, I nod. "Yes, please."

Keith returns with a can of whipped cream.

As he sits down beside me, he gestures to the gift. "You didn't open it yet? Get after it, tear into it."

While he dresses his pancakes, I open the gift.

When I remove the lid from the small box, my heart soars. "Christmas scrunchies! How did you know?"

He blushes as he smirks. "Well, your hair always seems to slip out of the ones you have. So I thought maybe the elastic was getting old. I figured a fresh batch would work better for you." A flash of worry creases his brow. "I mean, I like your hair down, but I'm sure it gets in the way at the bakery."

Running my fingers through my unruly red hair, my cheeks turn a matching shade. "You like it down?"

His bright eyes take in all of me before darting to his plate. "I like it anyway you have it. Truth is, I like you."

He reaches for a piece of fudge, unwraps it, and pops it in his mouth. "Wow! That's delicious."

"Really? You like it?"

"I love everything you make, Cindy. You're amazingly talented. But this may be my new favorite."

An embarrassment of compliments colors my cheeks as I slather my pancakes with syrup.

There's a comfortable quiet between us as we enjoy our breakfast. When I look up to pay him a compliment, I catch sight of the life-sized, hand-made birch-handled broom hanging on the wall above his sofa. The single gold-dipped twig among the broomcorns nearly stops my heart.

It's exactly like the pin Violet wore on her tunic.

Keith sets his fork on his plate and cranes his neck as he follows my gaze. "Oh, you noticed the broom. What do you think?"

My voice is trapped behind the knot in my throat. Poking absently at the pancakes, I set my fork down as a sudden loss of appetite sends a cramp through my stomach.

"Medical investigators don't get much opportunity to work on the living, Cindy. You don't look well. Is something wrong with the pancakes?" Cinnamon Roll's parting words about "what now" dance through my head. I have to be more careful.

The innocence of my North Pole upbringing has been shattered. No more ignoring my hunches.

"Where did you get that — that broom?"

"That's a real beauty, isn't it?"

"Where did you get it?" Anger creeps into my tone.

Keith wipes his mouth and pushes his chair back. When he gets to his feet, I sense something different about him. Is it all in my imagination?

"Keith, I need you to answer the question."

He walks toward the broom and my heart thumps in my chest.

A yip from the hallway confirms my suspicions. Without waiting for an answer, I dart out of Keith's apartment and fumble with my keys.

Artikoa takes a protective stance between me and Keith as I struggle to get my key in the lock.

The key finally slips into the lock, but the hair on my arms stands on end as the air fills with an electrical charge.

I know that sensation. Despite the fear and uncertainty, I don't want Artikoa to transform into his protective form and injure Keith. There's a flicker of doubt in my heart, and I—

"Artikoa, do not hurt Keith."

Through the open doorway, I see the hurt look on Keith's face. There's also something more, something I can't explain.

I shove my apartment door open and command Artikoa to follow me inside.

The wise elder does not immediately respond.

"Most Venerable Elder, your princess commands you. Return to the apartment at once."

Arti backs toward me. He's forced to obey my command, but he's clearly not overjoyed about it.

As I push the door closed, Keith's gaze drops to the floor, and his shoulders slump.

I lock the handle, the deadbolt, and slide the security panel over the doggy door. As I lean against my door, trying to catch my breath, part of me still fears the cloven hoof of a Krampus could splinter through the wood any moment.

Arti's hackles remain raised as he paces in front of me. "A birchwood broom with a gilded twig? You know what that symbol means, Cynthia. You've heard the tales. You saw the pin that Violet wore, and you should know better. You've been to his apartment before. Didn't you notice the broom?"

"I saw it, but I didn't think anything of it. People have all sorts of interesting decorations. You know how strange humans can be."

The stern fox slowly glances upward. "If he had attacked, no command on earth would have stopped me from protecting you."

Crouching, I stroke the fox's soft fur. "I know.

And I'm so grateful that you watch over me." My heart aches in my chest as my hand drops to the floor. "Something doesn't add up."

He moves between me and the door, still in protector mode.

"In my previous encounters with Krampus creatures, even in their human — or elf — form, they've exuded hatred or fear. Either they can barely bring themselves to spit my name out of their mouth or, like Violet, they couldn't even look at me."

Artikoa sits in front of the door, clearly committed to his post. "True. However, they are a large clan, and two encounters are hardly enough to create a data set, Your Highness."

"Fair enough." The images somersaulting through my mind of Keith are all good. "But what about his kindness, and the feeling of him believing me when no one else would? Plus, Keith gives me gifts and spends time with me. It doesn't make sense."

Arti's sharp nose points upward. "Perhaps he is the cleverest Krampus of all. He has gotten you to let your guard down. You were alone, in his lair. Anything could've happened."

Icy fingers seem to grip my shoulder. "How could I have been so wrong?"

. . .

I BARELY SLEEP A WINK. After I can no longer handle the tossing and turning, I roll out of bed, still wearing yesterday's outfit, and march into the bakery.

My ever-present guard in tow.

"Arti, you know you're not allowed in here."

In these wee hours before dawn, there's no one in earshot. "Cynthia, as long as we believe your life may be in danger, I will not leave your side. I will make myself unobtrusive in the back room of the bakery, but you cannot prevent me from doing my duty."

"Fine."

As usual, baking transports me into a world of happiness and peace. When Jasmine pokes her head into the back room, I'm genuinely surprised how much time has passed.

"You're here early, boss. Everything okay?"

The simple answer would be a lie, but I'm unable to fabricate one of those because of my pesky elf-blood. "Keith and I . . . I guess you'd call it a fight. I couldn't sleep."

Surprisingly, Jasmine walks toward me and slips an arm around my shoulders. "It's nothing to lose sleep over, Cindy. Happens to couples all the time. You'll work it out. He's a good guy."

The familiar sound of the espresso machine

bubbling and gurgling sends my mind off on its own adventure.

Keith *is* a good person. I didn't even give him a chance to explain. There has to be a reason why he wouldn't answer me. The scared little elf inside me whispers, "Yeah, he's a Krampus!"

What if he's not? What if I jumped to the wrong conclusion because of everything that happened at the North Pole?

"Arti? I may have misjudged Keith."

"Unlikely." He shrinks into the shadows between two large trash cans.

"Hey, boss, there's someone here to talk to you."

My heart thuds in my chest, and I can't seem to catch my breath. "Who is it?"

"It's Mitch, from the Piggly Wiggly."

The tension drains so quickly, my knees almost buckle. "Send him back."

"Hi, Cindy. I wanted to bring this by personally. After you and Cinnamon Roll asked about reindeer milk, I couldn't get it out of my head. There's a farmer up on Rural Route 26 that raises reindeer for Santa's Village."

"What? This far south? How does he get his reindeer to the dome?"

"Yip. Yip." Artikoa is on his feet.

Cracked candy canes! I've done it again.

There's no possible way Mitch is talking about Santa's actual village.

Mitch chuckles. "I love your sense of humor, Cindy. Anyway, here's a jug of reindeer milk. He says he probably has enough where he could spare a gallon a week if that helps you out."

"Thank you, Mitch. I'd love to try my *dulce de leche* sauce with reindeer milk." A soft grin lifts my cheeks. "Let your friend know how much I appreciate it. As long as no reindeer calves are going hungry, I could easily take a gallon a week."

Mitch chuckles and bobs his head. "That's just like you to be worried about the babies. I'll let him know. You have a great day and, if I don't see you, a happy New Year, eh?"

"Thanks, Mitch."

He wanders out front, and I stare at the jug of reindeer milk. Cinnamon Roll. She loves her original ingredients. Bless her heart for accidentally finding me a source. I'll have to send her a thank you the next time I talk to Mama.

After placing the special milk in the refrigerator, I untie my apron, and a mournful sigh escapes my lips. "I need a nap, Arti. Jasmine should be set for pastries until well after lunchtime. I'll let her know I'm heading upstairs."

"As you wish, Your Highness."

He sticks to me like peanut butter on a slice

of fresh bread as I make my way out of the bakery. Jasmine assures me she can handle everything for a few hours, and I stumble up to the apartment.

When I reach the landing between the two apartments, a wave of fear grips me, and I pause to stare at Keith's door with a mixture of worry and regret.

Arti bounds past me and draws my attention to a small box on the floor outside my door.

"It smells like Keith. I'll get rid of it."

"No. Wait." Crouching, I lift the box and remove the lid. The lovely set of Christmas hair scrunchies stare up at me with disappointment.

"Look, Arti." I tilt the box toward the fox. "Krampus wouldn't give me a Christmas present. After the horrible way I treated Keith, he still brought this present to my door. I'm sure I've misjudged him. What can I do? I've ruined everything."

The wise elder remains silent, but there's doubt in his all-knowing amber eyes. We enter the apartment in silence.

My brief nap is filled with strange visions. Some replay the events that transpired at the North Pole, others are new and horrible nightmares where Keith transforms into a terrifying beast.

Despite the fitful sleep, I feel a bit rested when I hop up.

Artikoa sits with his back against the door. Not totally convinced of Keith's innocence.

"I'm going down to the bakery. I honestly don't need you to watch over me. I'm right about Keith. I feel it."

Arti tilts his head first to one side and then the other. "I will remain in the apartment. But if I smell anything suspicious, I will burst into that bakery regardless of human health codes."

"Thanks, Arti."

CHAPTER 19

*J*asmine has everything well in hand when I return to the bakery. Both the main retail space and the overflow area are full. Silver Shoals is a popular tourist destination in the days between Christmas and New Year.

"Do you need anything in particular, Jazz?"

She gives the pastry case a once-over and shrugs. "The new head deputy at the station came down and complained that we didn't have any bear claws."

Bear claws were not something that we made at the North Pole, and I've paged through Connie's recipe books enough times to know she doesn't have any recipe for them either.

"Hmmm, I'll make them a *bûche de Noël*. Traditionally, they're not served after Christmas, but everyone loves them."

Jazz nods as I walk into the back room. The smile on my face evaporates when I think about delivering the Yule log cake to the place where Keith works.

Poking my head around the corner, I scrunch up my nose and ask, "Would you mind delivering it to the sheriff's station?"

Her knowing gaze carries sympathy and understanding. "No problem, boss."

The recipe is probably older than my father. I remember making dozens of them with Cinnamon Roll every year. Each elf clan has slightly different holiday traditions, but there were several that insisted on the *bûche de Noël*.

Once I've assembled all the ingredients, I lose myself in the process of creation. My heart is heavier than usual, and my baking escape is frequently interrupted by thoughts of Keith.

Maybe I should deliver the cake? Nope. Bad idea. If he's upset with me, that's not a discussion I want to have in the middle of the station. Tapping my fingers on my bottom lip, I search for a better idea.

Got it! I'll make two mugs of hot chocolate after we close the bakery and cross my fingers that he stops by to tell me about his day.

The hours fly by, and, roughly an hour before closing, I finish the beautiful Yule log cake. "Jasmine! Jazz, the cake is ready."

She unties her apron, slips it off, and tosses it into the laundry hamper. "That's gorgeous, boss. You really have some kind of magic when it comes to baking."

The blush hums across my cheeks as I realize how close she's come to the truth. "Aw, thanks. And especially thanks for delivering this for me."

Jasmine carefully places the cake in a large green pastry box, bundles up against the cold weather, and turns to leave. "I should be back in about a half an hour to help you close."

"No need. I'll handle things here and close up. You should probably take a couple days off. I know we didn't close on Christmas like we have in the past. Cinnamon Roll loves to work."

Jasmine balances the cake precariously in one hand while she ticks her finger back and forth like a metronome. "You know, how about if we close on New Year's Eve and New Year's Day, instead?"

New Year's isn't a holiday celebrated at the North Pole. For us the new year begins the day after Christmas, but I'm learning to embrace human customs. "That sounds perfect. I'll see you tomorrow."

"Tomorrow, boss." She waves to a few regulars as she heads out the door.

My apron is a disaster, but our patrons always tell me how much they love knowing everything is made on site and not shipped in a refrigerated truck, so I proudly walk behind the counter.

Traffic tapers, and our guests finish their treats. A few buy more to take home, and I lock the exterior door in the foyer. Cleanup is easier if I leave the overflow seating area on the other side of the foyer and the retail space unlocked.

Sweeping, mopping, and wiping down tables takes my mind off my cracked heart.

Eventually, I whip up two mugs of peppermint hot chocolate, and plant myself at the table closest to the front door.

My cocoa is long gone and the darkness outside deepens. No sign of Keith. He probably has a case. I'm not going to read too much into it.

The days simply melt into one another.

Up early, making the dough, baking the cookies, afternoon break, and more baking.

Each night after closing the shop, I sit at the table until the second mug of hot chocolate turns ice cold.

By December 30th, I've given up. Whatever I've done, I've hurt Keith beyond repair. I don't blame him. There's no explanation for treating him like a criminal, especially having only the tiniest piece of evidence.

After securing the bakery, I trudge upstairs and mope into the apartment. Artikoa's pointed little ears angle together. "Still no sign of Mr. Winters?"

"Nope. He's up before me and coming home long after I'm in bed. If he even is coming home. You know how good my hearing is, and I haven't heard a peep from that apartment since — since the fight."

The fox shakes his head back and forth. "Not true, Cynthia. I've heard him come and go. But he employs the stealth of a crafty predator. I'm not sure that proves innocence of any kind."

Throwing my hands in the air, I exhale as tears burst from my eyes. "He's not a predator. He's a good person. A totally human person. And he's on the Nice List! I know that in my heart. I'm going to write him an apology and leave it outside his door."

Taking the notepad and pen from my counter, I attempt to craft a proper apology. Each time I make a mistake or phrase something the wrong way, I crumple up the note and toss it on the floor.

As the pile of paper balls grows, Arti hops onto the green-velvet chair opposite me and glances at my notepad. "I don't approve of this idea, but I'll never get a wink of sleep with all this crinkling of paper." A flicker of compassion touches his gaze. "Don't try to cover everything. Simply apologize for leaving without an explanation and inform him you wish to discuss things further. Offer a place and time. And leave it at that. If he wishes to provide his own explanation, he will be at the place you specify."

"Thank you. Thank you, wise Elder."

He sniffs sharply, curls into a tight ball, and lays his thick fluffy tail over his eyes.

Taking his advice, I offer a simple apology and inform Keith that my bakery will be closed on New Year's Day. I mention that I'll be in the bakery with a fresh Yule log cake and two mugs of peppermint hot chocolate at 10:00 a.m.

After folding the letter, I cautiously open my front door, tiptoe across the hallway, and slide the note under his door.

Sleep continues to evade me, although tonight is at least devoid of nightmares.

On New Year's Eve, the bakery provides a welcome distraction. Jasmine and I place a sign up indicating the bakery will close at noon.

No one seems to have a problem with it. Many of our customers purchase items to take home for various parties they're either hosting or attending.

"Hey, Jazz, I forgot to ask you what happened when you delivered the Yule log cake?"

She pauses and makes a grand production of having to think back so many days. "Let's see. The deputy at the front desk actually squealed. Then she made an announcement over the loudspeaker. After that, that new head deputy — I think her name is Paulsen — came out with her hand on her gun. She looked like she was about to throw me in jail."

"What? Oh dear! I'm so sorry—"

"No. No. Once she caught sight of the cake, everything was fine. She ushered me into their break room and took the first slice for herself. She may not be the most thoughtful deputy, but it sounds like she's in charge of the whole place now. Deputy Rivera had to take family leave to head back to New Mexico and care for an ailing parent."

"I'm so sorry to hear that. Will he be back?"

Jazz shakes her head. "Doesn't sound like it."

Rocking back and forth on my feet, I bite my lower lip and search for the proper phrasing.

Jasmine steps closer. "If you're wondering about Keith, I didn't see him. He may have been there, but he didn't come into the break room."

"Oh. Then I'll make another Yule log cake and I'll sit here waiting for him all day tomorrow, if I have to. I'm going to apologize to him, whether he likes it or not."

Jasmine laughs until she snorts. "That's the spirit, boss. I'll see you on January 2nd."

"Happy New Year, Jasmine."

"Same to you."

After closing the bakery, I spend the rest of the day crafting the most beautiful Yule log cake I've ever made. I roll the cake lengthwise to create a thick stump version, and turn it on its end.

Next I make dark chocolate shards to mimic bark. The cake is gorgeous, but it needs a scene. Using fondant, gum paste, and marzipan, I create a perfect North Pole scene. Santa chatting with Rudolph, and two elves washing the sleigh.

Placing the cake in one of the large refrigerators, I sulk upstairs, dreading the long night ahead.

When I enter the apartment, Artikoa is nowhere to be seen.

Loneliness has its claws so deep in my heart that I'm actually considering a snow globe call to my mother — for no reason.

As I approach the snow globe on my bedside table, a small golden scroll catches my eye. "The ritual!"

This is the perfect night. Everyone will be busy, and I will be alone in the bakery.

"How wonderful!" Clutching the scroll, I hurry back to the bakery, unfurl the parchment, and study the precious ritual.

CHAPTER 20

*M*ama was kind enough to list all the supplies I would need at the top of the parchment. After a quick review, I'm hoping I have everything I'll need.

- Star anise
- Rosemary
- Whole clove
- Cinnamon
- Mortar and pestle
- 1 lb of salt
- A loaf of bread (to offer the spirit nourishment)
- 3 candles
- A personal item that belonged to the deceased

- A dollop of love

MY MOTHER HAS BEAUTIFUL PENMANSHIP. In tiny calligraphy, she's added a note that, the more time the deceased has spent with the item when they were alive, the more effective it will be.

I'll start with the easiest item on the list — the personal item. Connie's cookbook. I know for a fact that she spent endless hours with her beloved recipes.

When setting up the bakery a couple of years ago, I ran across a drawer with candles, matches, and a small transistor radio. Artikoa told me that those items were used in case of a power outage or other type of human emergency. Since the North Pole is powered by magic, we haven't had any experience with blackouts.

A quick search of the drawers in the pantry reveals a stash of white candles. I grab three of the tea lights and set them on the counter beside Connie's cookbook.

Next, I need to locate the herbs and spices. Lucky for me, I'm at a bakery!

Carefully adding spices to the mortar and pestle, I crush and grind until everything is a nice powder.

Retrieving the one-pound bag of salt from the

pantry, I pour it into a large mixing bowl, add the ground spices, and stir.

The scroll doesn't mention anything about sweeping the floor, but it feels right to me. After sweeping the floor, I place the loaf of Connie's recipe rye bread on a tea towel and set the three candles on the floor.

Finally, I pour the large salt circle around the items and carefully step inside with the scroll. Taking the matches from the pocket of my hoodie, I light three candles and read the enchantment.

In the past, when I thought I'd felt Connie's spirit, she came on her own. Part of me worries she won't respond to a summons.

I have nowhere to be, so I read the enchantment two more times before tucking the scroll in my pocket.

Nothing happens.

Cookie crumbs! I don't have the magic of Christmas Eve on my side. Wait! The dollop of love. I can add more than a pinch of that.

Placing both hands on Connie's recipe book, I talk to her as though she were sitting across from me.

"Connie, your husband was the kindest human I ever knew."

My voice catches in my throat. A rush of relief flashes through my brain. I can say whatever I want to Connie's ghost. I don't have to keep any secrets from her.

"Connie, Santa Claus is my father. My mother is an elven queen. I grew up in a magical dome at the North Pole, and Ronnie was my first human friend."

The air stirs outside the circle, and my heart stutters.

"I've worked hard to fit in here in the human world. I've learned about money, slang, and sarcasm. But the thing that's meant the most to me is your recipes. The love you put into creating each of these special treats is something I can connect with easily. You loved baking the way I love baking. If you'd like to continue hanging out in this bakery and talking to me, I'm here for it."

The air outside the circle thickens, and my angel blood can sense a growing presence.

"I'd love to be your friend, Connie. I think ghosts and angels are natural friends, don't you?"

A soft voice wisps through the air. If not for my exceptional elven hearing, I may have missed it.

"Oh, you betcha. We'll be fast friends."

Focusing my eyes on the disturbance in the air, I whisper, "Connie? Is that you?"

Back-combed grey hair, snazzy red cat-eye glasses, and a homespun gingham apron take form. "Geez! I can't believe I'm meeting Santa's own daughter. I wish I could tell all the gals at bingo."

A flash of panic strikes before I remember she can't tell anyone. "Pleasure to meet you, Connie Schmenkel." Patting her beloved recipe book, I smile at the ghost. "This is a treasure. I'm not sure if you can communicate with Ronnie, but, if you can, please tell him how grateful I am for this gift."

She turns, and I marvel at the perfect bow on the back of her apron. Clearly tied with decades of practice and more than a dollop of love.

"Ronnie? Ronnie, get your skinny behind up here. This nice girl wants to talk to you."

The familiar face of Ronnie Schmenkel shimmers to life next to Connie.

"Ronnie! I thought I'd never see you—" Emotion steals my voice.

"Well, Cindy Claus. Did I hear you tellin' Connie you're Santa's actual daughter? I knew there was something special about you the first time I met you."

Ronnie looks healthy and peaceful. No four-prong cane, no labored breathing.

"I want you to know we caught the person who took your life. Me and Keith and Sven — we didn't rest until we solved the case."

He grins and slips an arm around Connie's shoulders. "Sure do appreciate that. Truth is, I'm doin' pretty darn good here. My heart broke in two the day this sweet gal crossed over. I'm content where I'm at, Cindy."

"So glad to hear it. I may as well tell you, my Papa bought the entire building from Sven after you crossed over. Santa paid him a handsome price and gave me the deed as a present last Christmas."

"Well, what do you know? Santa really does know exactly what everyone needs. How's things been working out for you, being Keith's landlord?" Ronnie smirks and gives a little wink.

A fresh set of tears bubble to the surface, and I press a hand to my aching chest. "We had a fight. I haven't seen him or talked to him all week."

Connie dusts invisible flour from her hands as she tilts her head toward her husband. "Don't you worry about a thing. Men are born pigheaded, raised pigheaded, and, if they're anything like this guy, they die pigheaded. The trick is to love them, anyway. I don't know what you and Keith disagreed about, but he'll be back. Don't you worry."

The freedom of being able to say anything I want is intoxicating. As I retell the story of the Krampus poisoning Santa, and the symbol of the birch-handled broom with the golden twig, Connie and Ronnie are enthralled.

When I end the story with the terrible scene in Keith's apartment, they both let out heavy sighs.

Ronnie nods. "I didn't work with Keith. He joined the force after I retired. But I never heard a bad thing about him. Better go with your gut, Cindy. I'm telling you, you've got an instinct for solving mysteries. This whole situation with Keith — it's just a mystery you need to solve."

Connie jumps in, "Don't worry about what you think is happening, just keep your side of the street clean."

The tilt of my head reminds me of Artikoa, and I wonder if I'll tell him about my ghostly encounter.

"What does that mean?"

Connie grips her husband's hand and gives it a squeeze. "It's real simple, you know? You make sure you're not bringing any extra trash to the party, and you count on Keith to do the same. You may have jumped to a conclusion, but he wasn't being honest with you. Like you said, he didn't give you an explanation."

"You're right. I kept asking him where he got the broom, and he didn't answer. If he had just answered—"

"Cindy? Who are you talking to?"

My heart leaps into my throat and, as I spin to face him, my hand wipes through the salt circle.

Connie and Ronnie disappear with a quiet snap of electricity.

Standing in the doorway to the back room of my bakery is the handsome and confused Keith Winters.

Hundreds of things race through my head faster than elves wrapping presents on the assembly line.

How did he get in?

How much did Keith hear?

Is he a Krampus?

Before I can open my mouth, a whisper trickles through the veil: "Keep your side of the street clean."

Getting to my feet, I walk toward Keith, desperately searching for the right thing to say.

I always imagined having to break the news to him I'm a quarter angel. Like that would be the biggest shock. Now I'm caught in the middle of whatever this ritual is, and I have to tell him I can talk to ghosts! Blizzards!

Keith shoves one hand in the pocket of his jeans and stares at the circle of items on the floor with the curiosity and keen eyes of a medical investigator. "Candles, a salt circle, a cookbook, and — is that a loaf of bread?"

All I can manage at this point is a brief nod.

He continues. "Don't worry, I've played with a Ouija board or two. Who are you trying to contact?"

"You're not freaked out?" I point to the floor. "I was— I wanted to talk to Connie."

He nods and exhales slowly. "After my grandma passed, I picked up a Ouija board at a garage sale, and got it out every night for two months. Nothing happened. I wanted it to. I believed with all my heart that it would, but nothing." He shifts his weight from one foot to the other. "Did you have any luck?"

Now would be a wonderful time to lie. No dice. The elf blood is too strong. "Yes. I talked to Connie and Ronnie."

Tears trickle down my cheeks. I can't think of another thing to say.

Keith steps closer and reaches out to wipe the tears from my cheek. Instead, I flinch.

His gentle green eyes flood with hurt. His hand drops to his side. "Cindy, I would never hurt you. I don't know why that broom scared you, but I'd like to talk about it. This past week has been — torture. I love chatting with you in the evenings and . . . Well, it's been rough without that touchstone."

My heart floods with love. Despite all of Artikoa's warnings, I can't help myself. I trust Keith Winters. Alone in the bakery in the middle of the night, I'm literally trusting him with my life.

Slipping my hand into his, I lead him to a table.

"Wait here. I'll make some cocoa and be right back."

He nods and slides onto a chair.

I return with two fresh mugs of hot cocoa, with candy cane spoons sticking out of each one. We stir our hot chocolate in silence, each watching our candy cane spoons melt into the chocolate goodness.

Keith is the first to speak. "I'll start with the elephant in the room. That broom."

I'm not sure what brooms and elephants have to do with each other, but it's probably more of that human slang.

"The broom is a family heirloom, but not *my* family's."

My ears perk up and I lean forward.

"After my grandmother passed, I went to live with Aunt Ethol and Uncle George. They weren't actually related to us, but they were lifelong friends of my grandmother and me. They had a big farm and no children of their own."

My heart is fluttering, and I can scarcely breathe.

"I grew up milking cows and collecting chicken eggs, and I even took a pig to the county fair. George and Ethol wanted more for me. The year I graduated from high school, they sold their dairy herd and gave me the money for college."

"So kind of them."

"It was. It was more than I had a right to. My freshman year, they both passed away in a strange accident. Evidence of a vehicle fire was found, but their bodies were never recovered." He sniffs sharply. "Their disappearance caused me to study even harder. I used all the money I got from selling the farmland and buildings to pursue my medical degree."

My time among the humans leads me to say, "I'm sorry for your loss."

"Thank you. Other than the truck fire, nothing else on the farm was damaged or stolen. That broom was the only thing I kept from the auctioneer. And he wanted it. Trust me." Keith scoffs. "He told me that was twenty-four-karat gold on that twig. But I remembered how it always had a place of honor in George and Ethol's home, and I couldn't bring myself to part with it."

My heart teeters on the razor's edge. Half is filled with relief that Keith isn't a Krampus, but the other half feels heavy with dread. In all likelihood, he was raised by a Krampus. He knows cousins or other relations of George and Ethol. He could accidentally lead one straight to me.

"That's terrible. Well, I guess part of it was good, but it's a very sad story. Sorry you lost your grandma, and George and Ethol. And I'm very sorry for running out of your apartment with no explanation."

He reaches across the table, and I slide my hand into his.

His brilliant green eyes stare deeply into my blue ones. "How about we agree to no more secrets, eh? If you can accept my weird family heirloom, and I'm okay with you talking to ghosts . . ." He squeezes my hand. "You can trust me, Cindy. You can always trust me."

The dread drains right out of my heart, and I feel as though I can float. I lean across the table, and my lips find his, and I know I've truly found my home away from home.

RECIPE: NORTH POLE LINZER COOKIES

This recipe is totally safe! Cindy Claus and Artikoa approved.

Ingredients

- 12 Tablespoons (170 grams) **unsalted butter**, softened
- ½ cup (100 grams) **granulated sugar**
- Grated rind (zest) of 1 **lemon**, or 1 teaspoon **cinnamon** (*zest for fruit filled – cinnamon for chocolate or caramel filled*)
- 1 large **egg yolk**
- 1 teaspoon **vanilla extract**
- ¼ teaspoon **almond extract**

- 1⅓ cups (160 grams) **unbleached all-purpose flour**
- ¾ cup (72 grams) **almond flour**
- ½ teaspoon **baking powder**
- ½ teaspoon fine **sea salt**
- **Raspberry jam**, for filling
- **Confectioners' sugar** or glazing sugar, for dusting

Instructions

1. Cream the butter, sugar, and zest (or cinnamon) until light and fluffy, scraping the bowl as needed, approx. 4 minutes. Add the yolk, vanilla and almond extracts, and beat until combined.
2. Meanwhile, whisk together the flour, almond flour, baking powder, and salt. Add the flour mixture to the egg mixture and blend until just combined. Be careful not to over-mix the batter.
3. Divide the dough in half. Press each half into a circle. Wrap in plastic wrap, and refrigerate both circles of dough until firm, about 1 hour.
4. On a floured surface, roll ONE-HALF of the dough to $1/8$" thick. Using a 2½" diameter cookie cutter, or your favorite

holiday shape of a similar size, cut out cookies. Transfer cookies to a parchment-lined baking sheet. Gather the dough remnants, roll, and repeat. If, at any point, the dough becomes sticky, wrap and refrigerate for 20 minutes – then re-roll.

5. Place the cut cookies (you should have 15 cookies) in the refrigerator for 30 minutes before baking.

6. Preheat the oven to 350°F (175°C).

7. While those cookies chill, cut 15 from the remaining dough using the same cutter/shape as the first half. Place the cookies on a baking sheet, using a small cutter or the circular end of a cake-decorating tip to cut a window in the center of each "top" cookie. Place this batch in the refrigerator for 30 minutes to chill.

8. Bake all of the cookies for 10 to 13 minutes, or until the edges are just beginning to turn brown. Let them cool on the tray for 5 minutes. Transfer to a rack to cool completely.

9. Place the cookies with the decorative windows in them on a sheet of parchment and sift confectioners' sugar

over the top. Turn the remaining cookies flat side up and spoon ½ teaspoon of jam into the center, spreading it slightly. Top with the powdered-sugar-dusted cookies.

Notes: To accommodate nut allergies, you can leave out the almond flour and substitute 3 Tablespoons (¼ cup or 32g) of cornstarch. Any lovely jam can be used for a filling. You could even try a chocolate spread or a thick *dulce de leche*.

How to store: Stack the sandwiched cookies in an airtight container, separated by parchment, on the counter or for 5+ days in the refrigerator. Freeze for up to 3 weeks.

To make in advance: You can prepare the dough, wrap it tightly in plastic wrap, and store it in the refrigerator for up to 1 week before cutting and assembling cookies. Let the dough sit at room temperature for approx. 20 minutes before rolling.

RECIPE: CHRISTMAS MINI CHOCOLATE-PECAN-CARAMEL CHEESECAKES

Cindy loves to make these tiny taste sensations for her papa. If they're good enough for Santa, your friends will devour them.

Yield: 24 servings
Ingredients
For the crumb crust:

- 24 **chocolate graham crackers** (full, rectangle crackers)
- 8 Tablespoons (114 grams) **unsalted butter**, melted
- ½ cup (100 grams) granulated **sugar**
- a pinch of **salt**

For the filling:

- Two 8-ounce (230 grams) blocks of **cream cheese**, softened (*don't use "whipped" style*)
- 8-ounces (230 grams) of **ricotta**
- 1 cup (200 grams) **granulated sugar**
- 2 large **eggs**
- 1 teaspoon **vanilla extract**
- 1 teaspoon **ground vanilla**
- ½ cup (118 ml) jarred ***dulce de leche*** (*See "Note" at end of recipe, if you want to make your own*)
- ½ cup (118 ml) **pecans**, chopped and toasted for topping

For the ganache:

- 12 ounces (340 grams) **dark chocolate**, roughly chopped
- ¾ cup (175 ml) **heavy cream**

Instructions

1. Preheat oven to 350°F/175°C. Line your muffin tins with cupcake liners. Recipe makes 24 mini cheesecakes.

2. To make the crumb crust, break the chocolate graham crackers into smaller pieces and place in a food processor and process to fine crumbs (or place in a plastic bag and crush with a rolling pin). Add the melted butter, sugar, and salt. Pulse — or mix thoroughly with a fork — until well combined, but not doughy. Divide the crumb mixture between the prepared cupcake liners. Approximately 2 Tablespoons per cup, then press firmly.

3. To make the filling, place the cream cheese and ricotta in a mixer and beat with paddle attachment until no lumps remain. Add sugar and eggs. Mix until combined. Add both types of vanilla and 3 Tablespoons of *dulce de leche*. Mix until combined.

4. Divide the batter equally into the 24 cups. Approximately 3 Tablespoons per cup.

5. Bake until a butter knife inserted in the center comes out clean, approximately 20 minutes. Transfer to a rack to cool. Chill in the refrigerator for 2 hours.

6. For the ganache, place the chopped dark chocolate in a bowl. In a

microwave-safe bowl, heat the heavy cream for 1 to 2 minutes or until bubbles form around the edges. Pour over the dark chocolate and let sit for 2 to 3 minutes.

7. Starting slowly, mix the dark chocolate and heavy cream. Continue mixing until fully incorporated. Once combined, set aside until cool to the touch.

8. Place 2 teaspoons of the ganache on each mini cheesecake and sprinkle with toasted pecan pieces. Next, drizzle with the remaining *dulce de leche*.

9. Pop in the freezer for about an hour to set the topping. Allow to sit at room temperature for up to 20 minutes before serving.

Notes: To make your own *dulce de leche*: Bring 2-quarts of water to a boil. Remove the label from an UNOPENED can of sweetened condensed milk and carefully place in the boiling water. Reduce temperature to a low simmer and cover. Let the can of sweetened condensed milk simmer for 3½ to 4 hours. With tongs, you can shift the position of the can to prevent a hot spot. At the end of the 4 hours, remove the can and let it cool COMPLETELY.

*It is best to prepare this the day before.

How to store: In an airtight container, separate layers by parchment, and keep for 5+ days in the refrigerator. Freeze for up to 3 months.

RECIPE: CONNIE'S FAMOUS HOLIDAY FUDGE

You can whip up a batch of this tasty fudge as fast as Cindy Claus. Try the variation, too!

Yield: 30 squares
Ingredients

- Nonstick spray
- 2½ cups (125 grams) **mini marshmallows**
- 16 ounces (475 grams) **CandiQuik** (or similar) **chocolate flavored melting chocolate**
- ½ cup (60 grams) **creamy peanut butter**
- 1¼ cups (190 grams) **Spanish peanuts**

Instructions

1. Line a 9x9x2-inch baking dish with parchment paper. Spray parchment with nonstick spray.
2. Evenly sprinkle 1 cup of marshmallows over the bottom of the pan.
3. In a separate microwave-safe bowl, microwave the chocolate for 2 minutes. Stir until smooth. If lumps remain, microwave for 10 seconds and stir again. Continue at 10 second intervals until all lumps are gone and chocolate is smooth and creamy.
4. Add peanut butter to melted chocolate. Mix well.
5. Set aside ¼ cup EACH of the marshmallows, peanuts, and the chocolate mixture.
6. Combine remaining ingredients and blend well.
7. Pour fudge mixture over the marshmallows in the pan.
8. Evenly sprinkle the reserved marshmallows and nuts over the top of the fudge. Then drizzle the reserved chocolate mixture over all.
9. Refrigerate until firm.

10. Cut into 1½-inch squares.

Fun variations: Substitute vanilla buttercream frosting for the peanut butter and substitute chopped candy canes for the Spanish peanuts.

How to store: Store fudge in an airtight container at room temperature for up to 4 days. Separate layers with parchment paper.

How to freeze: If planning to make a large batch to freeze, place in single layers in an airtight container with sheets of parchment paper between. Store in the freezer for up to 3 months.

RECIPE: YULE LOG CAKE (BÛCHE DE NOËL)

Cindy made this festive cake for Keith on New Year's Day. Seems like it might hold special powers!

Ingredients
For the cake:

- ½ cup (60 grams) **sifted cake flour**
- ¼ cup (32 grams) **unsweetened cocoa powder**
- 1 teaspoon (4.8 grams) **baking powder**
- ¼ teaspoon (1.5 grams) **salt**
- ½ cup (100 grams) **castor sugar** (you can substitute erythritol)
- 3 **eggs**, separated
- ¼ cup **milk** (59 ml)

For the filling:

- 2 cups **whipped** cream (240 grams) (you can substitute a nondairy whipped cream)
- 2 Tablespoons (30 ml) **Chambord, Grand Marnier, or Frangelico liqueur** (if you prefer no alcohol, you can substitute 1 Tablespoon vanilla)
- ¼ cup (28 grams) **confectioners' sugar** (run through a sifter if you want to ensure no lumps)

For the ganache:

- ¼ cup (54 grams) **butter,** *softened to room temperature*
- 8 ounces **semisweet chocolate** (22 - 30 ml), melted
- 2 cups **heavy whipping cream** (480 ml)
- *You can use marzipan and food coloring to create small decorations

Instructions
Make the cake:

1. Preheat oven to 350°F/175°C. Grease a 15x10-inch jelly roll pan. Line the pan with parchment paper and then grease the parchment.

2. In a medium mixing bowl, whisk together the flour, unsweetened cocoa powder, baking powder, and salt. Set aside.

3. Cream 3 egg yolks and sugar together using a stand mixer fitted with the paddle attachment (or in a large mixing bowl with a hand mixer) on medium speed until light and fluffy, about 2 minutes.

4. Gradually add the dry ingredients and alternate with the milk. Beat on low speed until combined (the dough will be thin).

5. Before you beat the egg whites, make sure you have a clean bowl and use a clean whisk attachment. Beat on high until stiff peaks form. *TIP: To lighten the batter, add about one third of the egg whites to the mixed batter and fold until incorporated.

6. Add the remaining egg whites and fold in, being careful not to deflate the whites.

7. Bake for 10-12 minutes until edges are set and center springs back. DO NOT OVER BAKE. An overbaked cake will crack when you attempt to roll it.

8. Place a clean tea towel on the counter and dust with confectioners' sugar or unsweetened cocoa powder (depending on your taste preference). Turn the cake onto the tea towel. Peel off the parchment paper. Trim the edges to improve the appearance after rolling.

9. Beginning with the long edge, roll the cake — using the towel to help prevent cracking — and transfer seam-side down to a wire rack to cool for up to one hour.

10. When cool, unroll the cake and remove the tea towel. Spread the boozy whipped cream filling evenly over the cake, careful to keep about ¾ inch from the edges. Re-roll the Yule log and place, seam-side down, on a tray or platter.

Make the filling:

1. Using a large whisk, combine the

confectioners' sugar and the alcohol (or vanilla) with the **WHIPPED** cream.

Make the ganache:

1. In a medium saucepan, bring heavy whipping cream, melted chocolate, and butter to a slow boil over medium heat, stirring continuously until blended. (I prefer to use a double-boiler to prevent scorching.)
2. Spread this over the top and sides of the Yule log with an offset spatula. Allow the ganache to set before storing.

*TIP: To decorate, dust work surface with confectioners' sugar. Knead green food coloring into half of the marzipan until blended. Roll marzipan to a $1/8$-inch thickness. Using a small knife, cut out leaves. With the remaining marzipan, create snowmen or mushrooms. Dust with confectioners' sugar and decorate your Yule log with leaves and other holiday-themed marzipan creations.

End of Book 3

But, more mysteries await...

Curl up with another case from the Christmas
Catastrophe Mysteries series!

A NOTE FROM TRIXIE

I hope you'll share the holiday spirit with your friends and family — anytime of year! Thanks for being on the Nice List.

One of the best parts of bringing Cindy to life continues to be the wonderful feedback from early readers. Thank you to my alpha readers, Angel and Michael. HUGE thanks to my fantastic beta readers who give me extremely useful and honest feedback: Nadine Peterse-Vrijhof and Veronica McIntyre. And big hugs to the world's best ARC Team – Trixie's Mystery ARC Detectives!

Thank you to my dedicated editor Philip Newey! I love to get his perspective on a story. I'd also like to welcome Dione Benson aboard as our new proofreader! Any remaining errors are my own.

I love baking! When my grandmother passed, I was lucky enough to inherit her recipe box. What a treasure! It brings a smile to my face every time I'm able to share one of her special bakes with you.

Special thank you to Carter, for coming up with Cinnamon Roll's husband's name: Barrel :)

FUN FACT: I've actually "played" Santa!

My favorite line from this case: "Oh my stars, you will not believe how strange humans are!" -Cindy

If you enjoyed this mystery, you can find more of my humorous paranormal cozies in the Mitzy Moon Mysteries, Harper and Moon Investigations, the Magical Renaissance Faire Mysteries, and the Mysteries of Moonlight Manor

We're so glad you chose to visit Silver Shoals. Stay tuned for another Christmas Catastrophe.

Trixie Silvertale (September 2025)

CHOCOLATE CRINKLE COOKIE MURDER

When the Christmas Carnival returns, will our trusting baker be skating on thin ice?

Cindy Claus loves baking holiday treats for her Silver Shoals community. This season she's gearing up for a jolly new local tradition. Just as she's embracing this human celebration, a tragedy claims the life of a beloved local.

The new deputy deems it an accident, but Cindy suspects foul play. Before she can dig up any clues, a stranger arrives, jumps into the investigation, and now Mitzy Moon and Cindy Claus will have to find a way to work together...

Can Cindy and Mitzy unfreeze the clues before a killer gets away with cold-blooded murder?

Chocolate Crinkle Cookie Murder is the fourth

book in the festive paranormal cozy series, Christmas Catastrophe Mysteries. If you like kind-hearted heroines, furry sidekicks, and a dash of mistletoe magic, then you'll love Trixie Silvertale's wintery whodunit.

Buy *Chocolate Crinkle Cookie Murder* to crack this chilly case today!

Features recipes from Cindy's bakery, AND a guest appearance by Mitzy Moon and Erick Harper!

Grab your next read here!
readerlinks.com/l/5212657

Scan this QR Code with the camera on your phone. You'll be taken right to the next Christmas Catastrophe Mysteries *adventure!*

SPECIAL INVITATION . . .

In between Christmas Catastrophe Mysteries, you can come visit Pin Cherry Harbor!

Get access to the Exclusive Mitzy Moon Mysteries character quiz – free!

Find out which character you are in Pin Cherry Harbor and see if you have what it takes to be part of Mitzy's gang.

This quiz is only available to members of the Paranormal Cozy Club, Trixie Silvertale's readers group.

Visit the link below to join the Trixie's Club and get access to the quiz:

http://trixiesilvertale.com/paranormal-cozy-club/

Once you're in the Club, you'll also be the first to receive updates from Pin Cherry Harbor and access to giveaways, new release announcements, behind-the-scenes secrets, and much more!

Scan this QR Code with the camera on your phone. You'll be taken right to the page to join the Club!

THANK YOU!

Trying out a new book is always a risk and I'm thankful that you rolled the dice with Cindy Claus. If you loved the book, the sweetest thing you can do (*even sweeter than peppermint hot chocolate*) is to leave a review so that other readers will take a chance on Cindy and Artikoa.

Don't feel you have to write a book report. A brief comment like, "Can't wait to read the next book in this series!" will help potential readers make their choice.

Leave a quick review HERE
https://readerlinks.com/l/4689821

THANK YOU!

Thank you kindly, and I'll see you in Silver Shoals!

ALSO BY TRIXIE SILVERTALE

Mitzy Moon Mysteries

Fries and Alibis: Paranormal Cozy Mystery

Tattoos and Clues: Paranormal Cozy Mystery

Wings and Broken Things: Paranormal Cozy Mystery

Sparks and Landmarks: Paranormal Cozy Mystery

Charms and Firearms: Paranormal Cozy Mystery

Bars and Boxcars: Paranormal Cozy Mystery

Swords and Fallen Lords: Paranormal Cozy Mystery

Wakes and High Stakes: Paranormal Cozy Mystery

Tracks and Flashbacks: Paranormal Cozy Mystery

Lies and Pumpkin Pies: Paranormal Cozy Mystery

Hopes and Slippery Slopes: Paranormal Cozy Mystery

Hearts and Dark Arts: Paranormal Cozy Mystery

Dames and Deadly Games: Paranormal Cozy Mystery

Castaways and Longer Days: Paranormal Cozy Mystery

Schemes and Bad Dreams: Paranormal Cozy Mystery

Carols and Yule Perils: Paranormal Cozy Mystery

Dangers and Empty Mangers: Paranormal Cozy Mystery

Heists and Poltergeists: Paranormal Cozy Mystery

Blades and Bridesmaids: Paranormal Cozy Mystery

Scones and Tombstones: Paranormal Cozy Mystery

Vandals and Yule Scandals: Paranormal Cozy Mystery

Harper and Moon Investigations

Ropes and Last Hopes: Paranormal Cozy Mystery

Bells and Bombshells: Paranormal Cozy Mystery

Rodeo Clowns and Shakedowns: Paranormal Cozy Mystery

Stiffs and Petroglyphs: Paranormal Cozy Mystery

Fatal Wines and Valentines: Paranormal Cozy Mystery

April Curses and May Hearses: Paranormal Cozy Mystery

Wheels and Dirty Deals: Paranormal Cozy Mystery

Scripts and Empty Crypts: Paranormal Cozy Mystery

Christmas Catastrophe Mysteries

Peppermint Cookie Murder: Paranormal Cozy Mystery

Apple Dumpling Murder: Paranormal Cozy Mystery

Linzer Cookie Murder: Paranormal Cozy Mystery

Chocolate Crinkle Cookie Murder: Paranormal Cozy Mystery

...more to come!

MAGICAL RENAISSANCE FAIRE MYSTERIES

Explore the world of Coriander the Conjurer. A fortune-telling fairy with a heart of gold!

Book 1:

All Swell That Ends Spell – A dubious festival. A fatal swim. Can this fortune-telling fairy herald the true killer?

Book 2:

Fairy Wives of Windsor – A jolly Faire. A shocking murder. Can this furtive fairy outsmart the killer?

Book 3:

Double Double Royal Trouble – When a treat-peddling witch is found dead, will this cursed faire crumble?

MYSTERIES OF
MOONLIGHT MANOR

Join Sydney Coleman and her unruly ghosts, as they solve mysteries in a truly haunted mansion!

Book 1: ***Moonlight and Mischief*** – She's desperate for a fresh start, but is a mansion on sale too good to be true?

Book 2: ***Moonlight and Magic*** – A haunted Halloween tour seem like the perfect plan, until there's murder...

Book 3: ***Moonlight and Mayhem*** – An unwelcome visitor. A surprising past. Will her fire sale end in smoke?

ABOUT THE AUTHOR

USA TODAY Bestselling author Trixie Silvertale grew up reading an endless supply of Lilian Jackson Braun, Hardy Boys, and Nancy Drew novels. She loves the amateur sleuths in cozy mysteries and obsesses about all things paranormal. Those two passions unite in all her paranormal cozy mysteries, and she's thrilled to write them and share them with you.

When she's not consumed by writing, she bakes to fuel her creative engine and pulls weeds in her herb garden to clear her head (*and sometimes she pulls out her hair, but mostly weeds*).

Greetings are welcome:
trixie@trixiesilvertale.com

f facebook.com/TrixieSilvertale

○ instagram.com/trixiesilvertale

BB bookbub.com/authors/trixie-silvertale

www.ingramcontent.com/pod-product-compliance
Lightning Source LLC
Chambersburg PA
CBHW022009170626
46808CB00001B/346